Blame It On
The Mistletoe

Samantha Baca

Sugarplum Falls Series

Blame It On The Mistletoe

Blame It On The Eggnog

Blame It On The Candy Canes

Blame It On The Reindeer

Blame It On The Carols

Blame It On The Blizzard

Cover Design: Richard Baca
Image(s): DepositPhotos

Contents

One
Jackson

I opened the door to Sugarplum Cuts and stepped inside, gently guiding Sophie with my hand on her back. I could tell that she was nervous—hell, so was I. The salon was busy with almost all of the twelve seats filled with women getting their hair cut, colored, or styled.

I looked down at my niece, noticing the way she pulled her long sleeves over her hands and hid her face behind them. Her long blonde hair was a tangled mess that I'd been fighting with for over an hour, and I was at my wit's end. It was just one of several battles I'd lost over the past few weeks.

Christmas carols floated in the air around us as twinkling lights offered a soft ambiance, making it feel warm and cozy inside. A sugar cookie scented candle was burning at the reception desk, along with an elaborately decorated gingerbread house. But that was nothing compared to the plush tree decorated in the back of the salon or the beautiful paintings on the floor-to-ceiling windows with festive holiday scenes that Sophie was admiring.

"Can I help you?" A woman asked, walking up to the desk to greet us. She had the same uniform as the other employees, a pair of black dress pants and a white button-down shirt with a name tag that said, *Emily*.

1

She was slightly older than the other hair stylists, but her smile was warm and friendly, which immediately put me at ease. While the other stylists looked to be in their early twenties and sported vibrant colored hair, Emily wore hers in a short cut that barely brushed the back of her neck but had longer strands in front that were tucked behind her ear and swept across her forehead. I couldn't peg how old she was, but something about her made me think she was closer to my age than she was to her coworkers.

"Yes," I said softly, squeezing Sophie's shoulder reassuringly. I tried to focus on why we were there and not get lost in her emerald green eyes that made the Christmas tree look dim in comparison. "We seem to be having an issue with some tangles, and I'm completely lost on what to do. I was hoping someone might be able to help us."

Emily's eyes met mine, then she looked down at Sophie. Her face immediately softened as if she could somehow see the pain and grief etched on this sweet girl's face. She came around the corner and squatted in front of her.

"Hi, sweetie, what's your name?"

"Sophie," she whispered quietly.

"What a beautiful name for such a beautiful girl."

I felt my heart expand at how well she was handling her. I hadn't been a *parent*—it was still hard to think of myself that way—for long, but I was already protective over her, just as my sister had been. Hell, in the forty-two years I'd graced the Earth, I'd never had this level of responsibility in my life, and it was something that I didn't take lightly.

When I got the call a few weeks ago that my sister had been in an accident, my world stopped. I spent days in the hospital with her, waiting for her to pull through, but she never did. Aside from her daughter, I was the only family my sister had left, so it didn't surprise me that she'd named me the guardian for Sophie. Her father left the moment he found out he was going to be a dad, leaving my sister a single mom for the past five years.

"Do you want to come with me, and we can take a look at these naughty tangles?" Emily asked, extending her hand out.

Sophie looked up at me, and I nodded. She had been through so much in such a short period of time that I hated how uncertain she was about everything. She used to be the most confident kid who loved to be the center of attention, but now she chose to hide in the shadows in a world she no longer understood.

Emily helped Sophie into a chair by the sink and leaned over, taking in the mess she was about to work with.

"I'm really sorry," I said, clearing my throat of all the emotion that was building inside. I wasn't a soft guy, and emotion of any sort made me incredibly uncomfortable. "I'm very new to this and don't quite know what I'm doing yet."

"It's okay, we'll all learn together." She smiled a genuine smile that lit up her eyes and wrinkled the skin around them. "If you want to have a seat, be my guest." She nodded to the empty chair across from us.

I sat down and watched as her thin fingers softly moved through my niece's hair, earning her trust with each touch.

"Her hair is thick and a little coarse, so you'll want to start using a leave-in conditioner after washing her hair. It'll help manage the tangles and make them easier to comb through."

"Okay," I nodded and opened my phone to add another note to the list of things I was suddenly responsible for.

"Sophie, would it be okay if I washed your hair, so I can work on getting the tangles out? Then once that's done, we can pick a fun hairdo before you go."

She nodded and chewed her sleeve.

I relaxed the best I could in the chair and watched as Emily showed her the sink and let her feel the water before having her lean back so she could wash her hair. She was amazing with kids, and I felt even more insecure about my ability to raise one now. It was like she was a natural, and I couldn't even figure out the basics.

Once they washed her hair, Emily wrapped it in a fluffy towel and led her to another chair, where she began applying more stuff to her hair.

"You can use any leave-in conditioner you want, but I really like this one," she said, showing me the container she was using. "They sell it up front, but you can also get it at most drugstores for like a fraction of the price—but don't tell them I said that." She looked over her shoulder to make sure no one had heard.

"Thanks," I smiled. "I'll go ahead and grab some before I leave. I don't trust myself to remember the right one later."

I shoved my hands into my pockets and leaned against the post that separated her station from the next. We hadn't been there that long, but the majority of the seats were now empty. It had gotten quiet without all of the chatter. I glanced at my watch, checking the time. It was almost seven, and I imagined they were getting ready to close soon.

Emily worked diligently on combing through Sophie's hair, and I was in awe of how easily the tangles started to disappear. Once she had her hair tangle-free, she looked in the mirror and caught Sophie's eyes.

"Would you like me to do your hair for you?"

Sophie looked nervously at me.

"It's free of charge," Emily assured, finding my eyes in the mirror as she spoke.

"Thank you, that's not an issue." I turned my attention to Sophie and noticed the tears in her eyes. "Would you like her to do your hair?"

She nodded, and the tears fell harder.

Emily glanced at me, unsure of what to do.

I leaned in close and whispered so only she could hear me.

"Her mom passed away unexpectedly a week ago. She used to do her hair for her, and they had this special braid that I don't know how to do."

"I'm so sorry," she said softly, then walked around and leaned against the counter so she could see Sophie. "If you can tell me what the braid looked like that your mommy used to do, I'm sure I can do it for you."

"I don't know what it's called," Sophie whimpered, wiping her tear-stained cheeks.

"What if I showed you pictures? We can look through them and see if any of them look familiar."

Sophie nodded and squirmed in her chair.

I pulled up my calendar on my phone and looked at my schedule for the next few weeks. I had meetings piled up through Christmas, none of which would be easy to get out of. But I also knew that I needed someone to help teach me the ropes with doing Sophie's hair, and if that meant that I needed to schedule daily appointments with Emily, that's exactly what I would do. Sophie had been through enough already, and if I could make her life even a fraction of a bit better by having someone do her hair the way her mom used to, I would drop everything to make it happen.

They looked through a handful of images on Emily's phone until suddenly Sophie gasped and pointed to one.

"A fishtail! That's my favorite braid to do!" Emily gushed excitedly and smiled brightly at Sophie.

For the first time in days, I watched the smile spread across Sophie's face as Emily started pulling strands of hair together and braiding it.

Once she was done, she handed Sophie a handheld mirror so she could see the braid. She was still beaming, touching it gently with her fingers.

"Thank you," she said, jumping out of the chair and wrapping her arms around Emily's waist.

"It was my pleasure."

I looked around and noticed that everyone else had already left.

"I'm sorry we kept you late," I apologized as we walked to the front so I could pay. I pulled out my wallet and handed her my card, not worried about what it cost.

"It's not a problem," she assured me with a smile, then handed me the credit card receipt to sign.

I noticed that she had only charged for a basic wash and nothing else. I wanted to argue with her and ask her to run it again, but I'd already kept her long enough, so I kept my mouth shut and gave her a large tip for a $7 wash and bottle of leave-in conditioner.

When I passed the receipt back to her, she tucked it to the side and came around to walk us out.

"Oh, before we go, I was wondering if it would be alright if I scheduled a few appointments for the next few weeks until I get the hang of doing her hair."

"Sure, let's see what's available."

She grabbed an appointment book and pulled it out, thumbing to next week. It looked like they were open seven days a week, but there was no need for me to come back tomorrow. Monday would be the earliest, which would also be difficult given it would be my first day back to work after losing my sister.

"We have a handful of spots open, do you want morning, afternoon, or evening?" She looked up at me and waited.

"I was hoping that we might be able to see you again, and evening if possible. I don't want to keep you late again, but I'll take whatever the latest appointment you have that still gets you out on time."

She smiled and ran her finger down the page to her name. "I tend to take most of the walk-ins and don't really do appointments."

"Oh." I frowned and let my shoulders fall.

"I'm happy to schedule them for you," she laughed lightly. "I just meant that I'm pretty much free all the time because I don't take a lot of clients that come back to me. It's easier for me to do the walk-ins and let the other girls take the regulars."

"If you're sure you don't mind, I would love to schedule with you. I want someone Sophie will be comfortable with, and you already know what braid she likes."

She smiled again, and I felt like I couldn't get enough of it.

"Okay, well, I can do anytime next week. The latest would be six, as I have to get out of here by seven."

"Perfect. If you want to put us down for six every day next week, I would appreciate it."

"Every day?" She arched an eyebrow.

"It's a steep learning curve, and I'd really hate for her to have to go through the embarrassment of having her hair be that big of a mess again. Especially with her starting a new school."

She nodded and glanced at Sophie.

"Not a problem."

She filled in the book with my info and then handed me a card with the dates and times, not that I would forget. Sophie and I said goodbye, then walked out into the brisk evening air, feeling lighter than we did when we went in.

Two
Emily

"Sorry I'm late," I called as I rushed through the front door and slammed it behind me. I shivered from the bitter cold outside and took comfort in the warmth of the fire roaring in the living room.

I pulled my jacket off and hung it up, even though I knew I would just be turning around to put it on again in a few minutes. I was already running late, but I didn't want my girls to feel like I didn't have time to spend with them.

I rubbed my hands together, still trying to warm up, as I followed the smell of food to the kitchen. It was a little over three weeks until Christmas, and I still hadn't had a chance to put up any decorations, which felt like a sin in Sugarplum Falls. While it should be up to each resident to decide whether or not to decorate their house for the holidays, it wasn't. Sure, you could choose not to, but only if you wanted to be the gossip of a small town that was OBSESSED with Christmas.

I rounded the corner and found my mom standing at the stove, stirring a pot of macaroni and cheese while the kids washed their hands in the bathroom. Her silver hair was piled into a ponytail on her head as she wiped her hands on the Santa apron she was wearing around her waist.

"Sorry I'm late," I repeated now that she could hear me.

She smiled warmly and pulled me in for a hug.

"No worries. Dinner will be ready in a few minutes. What time are you going in tonight?"

I glanced at the clock on the stove and groaned.

"I'm supposed to be there in half an hour."

"Do you want to call and let them know you'll be a little late?"

"I can't. It's Saturday night, so it's going to be busy. Plus, I could really use the tips."

"I told you I'd help with Christmas this year," she sighed. "I don't like you working yourself this hard."

"I'm doing the best I can, Mom. Besides, it doesn't hurt the kids to see their mom work hard."

"No, but it would be nice for the kids to actually see their mom," she scolded, pointing the wooden spoon in my direction. "Working hard isn't a bad thing, but you need to balance your time with your family. Your kids are only going to be small for a short while. You'll blink, and they'll be grown up and won't need you anymore."

"I know, Mom." I leaned in and kissed her cheek. "But I really need the money, and I refuse to allow you to help me with this. You have enough on your plate with replacing a water heater and needing a new stove. If anything, I wish *I* could help you."

She leaned against the counter and studied me the way she always did when she thought I was overdoing it.

"I'm off tomorrow, so I plan on sleeping in with the girls, then decorating the house. I'm pretty sure I marked all the boxes when I put them away, so it should be easy to find everything."

"I'm sure they'll enjoy that."

"Do you want to join us? We can make a day out of it, then order dinner and have a game night." I grabbed a cold slice of pizza from the fridge and tossed it in the microwave.

"I'll clean it tomorrow," I laughed, already knowing what she was going to say about not covering the food that was sure to splatter.

She shook her head and swatted my butt playfully with the hand towel before hanging it over her shoulder.

"I have to run a few errands in the morning, but I can come by around noon."

"Perfect," I said around a mouthful of food.

A few minutes later, the girls came bouncing into the kitchen, wrapping their arms around me. Penelope was my oldest and almost as tall as me. She was nine but acted nineteen on most days, constantly making me worry about what her teen years would be like. Gracelyn just turned six and still acted like my little girl who loved Barbies and believed in the world of make belief and magic.

I felt my heart tug in my chest when I remembered Sophie. Her sadness washed over me in waves, and I could feel the pain flowing through her from losing her mother. I wanted to hold her in my arms and hug away the sadness. Her baby blue eyes sparkled when I'd braided her hair, and I couldn't help but notice the way her dad lingered protectively over her.

Jackson was unlike anyone I'd ever met before. Kind of gruff and protective but also sexy in a mysterious way. I wasn't sure if it was the gray eyes that got to me or the strong jawline and thin line of hair that dotted his jaw. His black hair was well-kept, and I would be willing to bet that he spent a lot of money getting it trimmed regularly. Or maybe it was just because he wore an expensive suit, rocked a Rolex, and left me an absurd tip on a basic wash. Either way, he screamed *made of money* without having to try.

"Are you going to be home with us tomorrow?" Gracelyn asked, looking up at me as she shoved a bite of macaroni into her mouth the second my mom set her bowl down in front of her.

I swallowed my bite of pizza and then washed it down with a drink of water before answering her.

"I sure am. I was just telling Nana that I thought we could put up decorations tomorrow, then order dinner and have a game night. What do you guys think?"

"Yay!" Gracelyn shrieked while Penelope shoved her macaroni around the plate, looking less enthusiastic about it.

"What's wrong?" I asked, sitting beside her.

"Nothing."

"Come on, Nel. Tell me what's wrong. Did something happen at school?"

Finally, she sighed heavily and pushed her plate away from her. She was in fourth grade but still hadn't adjusted to a new school or made many friends since she started. She was always my little independent girl and never one to be worried about whether people liked her or not. Penelope didn't look for anyone's approval, which was something that I admired about her, but I hated to see how much she struggled with social interactions at school.

"You were supposed to rehearse my lines with me when you got home today."

I closed my eyes and cursed under my breath.

"Honey, I'm so sorry." I reached over and squeezed her hand to get her attention. "I didn't forget."

"Yeah, right."

My mom looked over from the stove, and I held up my hand to stop her from saying anything. My mom helped me with the girls every day, and thankfully, she lived next door, so it wasn't out of her way to come by when I needed her. She was also aware of the new attitude problem Penelope had developed.

"First—don't take that tone with me. Second, I didn't do it on purpose, Nel. I got stuck working late at the salon, helping a little girl who needed me."

Her face softened slightly as she listened.

"What was wrong with her?" Gracelyn asked as my mother joined us at the table.

"Well, nothing was wrong with her. But she had these really bad tangles in her hair, just like you get."

"Did her mommy not know how to get them out?" Gracelyn pushed another bite into her mouth.

My throat burned as I swallowed past the lump that was forming.

"Her mommy recently passed away, and her dad doesn't know how to take care of her hair yet. He's learning but needed my help."

"Oh my," my mother commented, placing a hand over her heart.

I nodded.

"And now he knows how to do her hair?" Gracelyn asked, constantly full of questions.

"No, not yet. But he's scheduled appointments with me next week, so I can keep teaching him."

"Are you going to be late next week too?" Penelope asked.

"No. I scheduled them early enough to make sure I got out on time."

She nodded, then finally took a bite of her food.

"It sounds like you've made quite the impression on him," my mom noted.

"I really doubt that. I think he just felt comfortable with me handling his daughter. I can imagine how hard everything has been for him, and I'm sure he just needed someone who could step in and help for a moment," I said as I stood up and pushed my chair in, feeling the lump in my throat growing tighter.

I tossed my napkin in the trash and then washed my hands.

"I need to get going," I said, leaning down to kiss the top of the girls' heads. "Be good, and I'll see you in the morning. I love you both so much."

I bundled up and headed out to my car, thankful for the heated seats to keep me warm on my way to work.

I grew up in California, where it was constantly warm and sunny. I enjoyed my weekends on the beach, soaking up the warmth in my bones. That was where I met Mark, and we fell instantly in love. Within a few months, we'd moved in together, gotten engaged, then got married in a shotgun wedding when we found out I was pregnant with Penelope. He'd been the love of my life, and when he promised to love me for as long as he lived, we had no idea that cancer would cut that so short for us.

When Mark passed away nine months ago, I packed up the girls and moved to Sugarplum Falls with my mom. She'd been there for a few years and loved the small-town life. I had no idea what I was in for, but I needed something different. Something slower-paced would allow me to stop and catch my breath. The only problem was that I hadn't imagined how much Mark's medical bills would drain our accounts, and now I was busting my ass just to keep my head above water.

It wasn't easy finding well-paying jobs in a small town. So, I took what I could find, and my mom and I have been making it work since then. She helped out with the girls while I convinced myself that a better job would somehow magically appear. But soon, I'd have to grow up and stop believing in make-believe, just like Gracelyn. I was forty years old and struggling like a teenager who had no idea how to navigate their world.

Three
Jackson

The first week of getting Sophie adjusted to a new school was more challenging than I'd imagined, and the only saving grace through all of it was that her hair looked impeccable every morning when she went to school.

Emily had taken the time to show me how to touch up her hair in the morning, so we didn't have to worry about doing it again. Just a little bit of this balm instantly tamed the pesky little flyaways and looked like a fresh new braid.

I learned a lot that first week, which was a steep learning curve for all of us. I totally spaced making Sophie's lunch three days in a row and decided to just ask the school to keep my card on file so she could grab food on the days when I'd forgotten. They weren't surprised and said I wasn't the only single father to *forget* these things. I hadn't bothered to get into the details of how I was technically Sophie's uncle turned guardian-slash-father. It was too hard to process in my head, so I wasn't ready to explain it to anyone else at this point.

I hadn't even gotten around to telling Emily I wasn't Sophie's father. Not like there was a good opportunity to just blurt the news out, but I also hated the gnawing feeling that I was keeping something from her.

Plus, it wasn't like it was the right place or time to have that kind of conversation with her. While Emily was a really nice woman, it wasn't like we were getting to know each other while Sophie and I were there. It was a quick appointment for her to help with Sophie's hair and teach me how to manage it so I wouldn't have to keep taking her in every week.

But it also wasn't like I hadn't thought about asking Emily if she wanted to hang out sometime outside of the salon. There was something about her that made me want to get to know her. The way she laughed at Sophie's jokes or how her eyes lit up when she listened to her tell a story—those were the things I couldn't get enough of. Seeing her so engaged in what a five-year-old was saying felt addictive to me, and I wondered if she would give me the same attention if we had the opportunity to talk.

It was two and a half weeks until Christmas, and I was up to my eyeballs with contracts I needed to finish. On top of that, I still needed to do some Christmas shopping and decorate the house, or I was going to be the talk of Sugarplum Falls.

I hadn't lived there for long, but I quickly learned that the residents of Sugarplum Falls took Christmas VERY seriously, and it was a big deal that I hadn't hung lights or added any festive decorations outside. It was strange to see how obsessed this town was with Christmas, but then I reminded myself that I actually enjoyed walking down Main Street and seeing the hanging lights and murals painted on the windows of the shops.

My day was winding down, and I was looking forward to getting Sophie and taking her to Emily for her next appointment. This was our last week of scheduled appointments, and I felt the sting of disappointment when I knew that we wouldn't see Emily anymore unless it was randomly in town.

I was packing up my stuff for the day when Frankie, one

of the assistants from human resources, came in and set a stack of files down on my desk.

"What's that?" I asked, nodding to the pile as I slipped my coat on.

"That is the file for the company holiday party and the Sugarplum Falls Frosty Fest we signed up to host a booth for."

"Okay, and what are they doing in my office?" I was the CEO of the company, which meant I didn't handle these things, so it made no sense why she was bringing them to me.

"Bea said to give them to you since Justine just walked out and quit." She lifted her shoulders to her ears and winced as if she expected me to yell at her.

I pinched the bridge of my nose between my fingers and closed my eyes.

"What?"

"Justine quit."

I exhaled slowly and found her looking at me sympathetically when I opened my eyes.

"My assistant, Justine?"

She nodded.

I rolled my head on the back of my neck and groaned. This was the last thing that I needed right now.

"Tell Bea to find me a new assistant and to get someone else to take over this," I snapped, pointing at the stack.

"I'm sorry, Mr. Mason," she apologized. "I'm just doing what I was told." She turned and hurried out of my office before I could say anything more.

I groaned, knowing I would need to sit down with Bea first thing in the morning and get this straightened out. She was the President of Human Resources, but I was still her boss. For now, I had other priorities, which included picking Sophie up and getting her to her hair appointment with Emily.

By the time we got there, my mood was even more sour after I received a flood of emails that had been sent to Justine and redirected to me. I tapped my foot on the tile floor in frustration as I read through each one, trying to sort them in order of importance while Emily put a new braid in Sophie's hair.

"What's the matter?" she asked, looking up at me under a strand of hair she lifted with a comb before tucking it between two other strands.

"Nothing."

I didn't want to be a jerk, but nothing was going to improve my mood right now. I desperately needed a new assistant and definitely wouldn't have time to get someone trained and up to speed before everything was due in two weeks.

On top of the stress of getting seven contracts out, I now had to learn how to plan a holiday party and put together something for the Sugarplum Falls Frosty Fest. It was my first year spending Christmas in Sugarplum Falls, and while I had no idea what to expect from the annual festival, I'd heard enough talk around town to know that this was a huge event and something I couldn't afford to screw up.

"You know you don't hide it very well," Emily commented with a grin, nodding toward my foot that was still tapping next to the chair Sophie was sitting in.

I sighed heavily, set my phone back in my pocket, and folded my arms over my chest.

"My assistant quit today and left me with a massive pile of shit to deal with."

Her eyes widened as Sophie's head whipped up to look at me.

"Sorry," I apologized, offering her a sheepish smile. "I'm still learning."

Sophie giggled and returned to the Christmas book she was looking at while Emily turned her to the side and continued working on the other braid.

"Did you not use to curse around her before?" Emily asked quietly as her fingers moved rapidly through her hair.

"I honestly don't remember." I shoved a hand through my hair. "I've never paid attention until now."

Emily frowned but kept working.

"What's that look for?" I asked curiously, extending my legs in front of me and crossing one ankle over the other while sitting on the edge of the empty seat across from them.

"Nothing."

"Now who's the terrible liar?"

She caught me watching her in the mirror and raised an eyebrow.

"Fine," she laughed. "I just thought it was odd that you don't remember if you've cussed around her before now. It just seems strange that you wouldn't remember something like that."

I lifted my shoulders and then let them fall.

"I guess I didn't pay that much attention when I was there. Usually, my sister kept everything in line, so there wasn't much for me to be upset about, so I guess I probably didn't curse much around her until now."

"Did your sister live with you guys?" She tilted her head and lowered her eyes to focus on the thin strands of hair she was working with.

"No, they lived on their own, and I had my own place. We used to all live in New York City, but I moved to Sugarplum Falls six months ago for a job."

"Oh."

She was still frowning when it finally dawned on me that she didn't know Sophie wasn't my daughter. It hadn't come up before now, but it was also as good of a time as any to tell her.

"Sorry, I should have explained," I started. "Sophie is my niece. Her mom was my sister. I became her guardian after she…."

Emily stopped moving and closed her eyes.

"I'm so sorry, I just assumed."

"It's fine," I held up my hand. "It would be easy to."

Emily finished the braid and then sprayed something on Sophie's hair before stepping back and looking at her in the mirror. Sophie's eyes lit up as she caught sight of herself, her tiny fingers gently touching her hair.

"You look beautiful," I said, standing beside her.

"Thank you."

"You ready to go?"

Sophie nodded and got out of the chair while Emily held it to keep it from spinning under her.

We headed to the register to pay, just like we did every night, but tonight felt different.

It was earlier than usual, so I decided to do something I'd never done before.

"So, um, we were going to go grab some pizza for dinner," I said nervously, watching as Emily's brown eyes lifted to mine. "Would you like to join us?"

She smiled and tapped buttons on the credit card machine before tearing off the paper receipt and sliding it over to me.

"I'm sorry, I can't. But thank you for the offer."

I swallowed hard and scribbled my name on the signature line after leaving another ridiculously large tip.

"Sorry, I should've assumed you were seeing someone. I didn't mean to offend you."

"You didn't," she said quickly, tucking the receipt into the cash register. "I'm not seeing anyone, but I have to work tonight."

I glanced at my watch.

"Isn't it almost closing time?"

"It is here," she laughed. "But I start my other job in an hour. I'm a waitress at Sugar Faced Bar."

I shook my head and chuckled, still unable to get over the names of the businesses in town.

"You work two jobs?"

She nodded and pulled her mouth to the side.

"I would work three if it would let me get ahead. But then again, I wouldn't have any time to spend with my kids, and I'd hate that even more."

I pulled my head back in surprise.

"You have children?"

"Two girls."

It felt like I was learning so much about her, yet it wasn't enough. I wanted to know everything.

"I had no idea. Now I feel like a jackass for not asking you anything personal in the week we've been coming in every day."

"It's no big deal," she laughed again. "My girls are nine and six. My mom lives next door to me, so she's able to watch them while I work, but lately, I've been working so much that I hardly see them. It's kinda killing the holiday vibe I was trying to set for them. You know, Sugarplum Falls is huge on the holiday spirit," she joked.

"Tell me about it," I snorted, remembering that I still needed to decorate and start my shopping. Not that I had anyone other than Sophie to shop for, given that I had no family and very few friends.

"Well, have a good night, and I'll see you guys tomorrow. And Sophie, don't forget to look through that book I gave you and let me know what you decide for the pageant, okay?"

Sophie smiled and held the booklet to her chest, then nodded in agreement.

"Pageant?" I asked, furrowing my brow.

"You didn't know there was a school pageant?"

I shook my head.

"It's next weekend at the school. Sophie was telling me that she's one of the singing angels, so I offered to do her hair for her. My youngest, Gracelyn, is one too, so I can do both of their hair before the event if you'd like."

"Sounds great, thank you," I pushed out, trying to keep the mounting frustration out of my tone. "See you tomorrow."

I guided Sophie out of the salon and tried to figure out how I was going to manage the million things that were all needing my attention.

BLAME IT ON THE MISTLETOE

Four
Emily

I couldn't get Jackson out of my head over the next few days. When he'd come in to get Sophie's hair done, he'd been so distracted and busy with work that he'd kept his head down and stared at his phone the entire time. When he wasn't responding to emails, he was pacing the back of the salon, growling at people on the phone.

Jackson didn't strike me as a grumpy or demanding person but seeing him this stressed out gave me a different insight into him. It was like he was barely hanging on, and I was nervous that he would crash soon. I could tell he was very generous by the large tips he'd been leaving me since he started coming to see me for Sophie's hair, but that wasn't what I looked forward to the most when they walked through the door lately.

Today was already Tuesday, which meant that they only had three more days of coming in to see me. I'd offered to do her hair for the pageant on Saturday because I'd felt desperate for an excuse to see them again. Not just Jackson but Sophie too. She'd already left a mark on my heart, and the thought of not seeing her beautiful smiling face or hearing her tell stories broke me inside.

Thanks to the big tips he'd been leaving, I'd been able to decrease the hours I went to the bar, which gave me a little more time at home with the girls in the evenings before they went to bed. I still hated working so much and having to figure out how to balance my time without spreading myself too thin, but it was the best I could do right now.

When they came in tonight, Jackson seemed even more agitated than normal, his gray eyes almost as dark as his suit.

"Are you okay?" I asked over the water as I washed Sophie's hair. "You seem really irritated and upset today."

"I'm fine," he groaned. "My HR department is supposed to be finding me a new assistant, but apparently, no one in Sugarplum Falls is looking for work right now, so we have zero candidates and a million things that are falling on me."

"What kind of work is it?" I squirted some conditioner in my hand and then massaged it through Sophie's hair, focusing on the nape of her neck, where she seemed to get the most tangles.

"General administrative stuff. Answering phones, scheduling appointments, filing, that sort of stuff."

"And you guys can't find anyone willing to do it? Does the pay suck or something?"

I didn't mean to sound so condescending, but I couldn't believe that it was that hard for them to fill such an easy position.

He folded his arms over his chest and studied me.

"The pay is comparable, and the benefits are stellar."

"Then I don't see why it's so hard to find someone," I muttered. "Lord knows there aren't that many great jobs in Sugarplum Falls."

I felt the heat of his gaze as it settled on me.

"Do you know someone who is looking?" he asked.

I shook my head and lifted the sprayer to rinse Sophie's hair.

"No, just saying that jobs are hard to find here, that's all."

"Is that why you're still working two?"

His tone was gentle and sincere, which put me more at ease.

"I came from California and was used to having a second income to support us before my husband passed. Now I'm struggling to make ends meet with two jobs and a lower mortgage. It's crazy because I was supposed to catch a break by moving here, yet *I* feel like the one who's going to break."

I felt a shiver run through me and instantly regretted telling him so much. I didn't want his pity or to see the softness in the way he was looking at me.

"I'm sorry about your husband," he said softly.

"Thank you."

We didn't talk anymore about Mark or shitty jobs while I combed and dried Sophie's hair for her. She'd decided she wanted a break from wearing braids, so I was teaching her how to brush her hair with a different comb to help get the tangles out in the morning. I also made sure Jackson was paying attention since she wasn't going to be able to reach the back where most of them built up to begin with.

Before I knew it, we were done, and I was walking them to the register again, though I wasn't ready for them to leave. I'd grown to enjoy their company, and that made me worried that I'd gotten too close to them already.

I entered everything into the computer and then reached for

Jackson's credit card right as he pulled it away.

"Do you like working here?" he asked out of the blue.

I shrugged and thought about it.

"It's fine. Pays the bills."

"But do you *like* it?"

I let out a nervous laugh and shifted my weight behind the register.

"I don't know, I guess. Why?"

He looked at Sophie standing by the window, watching the snow fall outside.

"Because I want to offer you a job."

My brows shot up as my jaw dropped.

"What?" I stammered, knowing I must have heard him wrong.

"A job as my assistant."

I shook my head as my eyes wildly scanned the room, looking for one of those hidden camera crews that would pop out and tell you it was all a big joke.

"You're crazy," I laughed.

"Maybe," he shrugged. "That's a possibility. But I'm serious. Come work for me. I can guarantee that the pay is better than you make here."

"You don't even know what I make here." I folded my arms over my chest.

"Tell me, and I'll double it."

My eyes opened even wider.

"You are certifiably crazy. No wonder your HR department is having a hard time finding you an assistant," I joked. "You can't just offer random people jobs and decide what to pay them."

"Sure I can."

I rolled my eyes and felt the heat that was spreading through me. Just entertaining the thought of taking a job that paid double what I made here was insane. I would jump on that faster than a kid in a candy store.

"No, you can't. Don't be silly."

"Wanna bet?"

He locked eyes and pinned me with a look as he pulled his cell phone out of his pocket, dialed a number, and then held it to his ear.

"What are you doing?" I whispered.

He lifted a finger to silence me and then moved the mouthpiece as he spoke.

"Bea, I need you to draw up new hire paperwork for an administrative assistant," he said authoritatively. He listened as she spoke, then moved the phone to talk to me.

"What do you make here?" he asked.

"I'm not telling you that," I scoffed.

He raised a brow and then spoke directly into the phone again.

"Starting pay is forty dollars an hour with paid leave from Christmas Eve to January 2nd. Emily will report directly to me and will start tomorrow morning. I'll send her up to your office when she arrives at eight-thirty."

He finished his call while I stood there, my heart hammering out of my chest.

"Will that cover what you're making between both jobs?" he asked as he tucked his phone into his trouser pocket.

"Yes," I stammered, staring at him in disbelief. "But Jackson, you can't do that."

"Why not?"

"Because it's totally crazy!"

"We've already established your feelings on that." He winked.

"I can't just quit my jobs and work for you."

"Why not?"

I struggled to come up with a good excuse which seemed to please him as he grinned smugly at me.

"It's a win-win situation, Emily. I need an assistant, and you want a better-paying job. You've said that you wanted to spend more time with your kids, so this gives you nights and weekends free."

"You don't even know if I'm a good fit for the position," I protested. "What if I can't do the things that you need me to? I don't even know what kind of company it is!"

"It's a highly sought advertising company," he said proudly.

"But I don't know anything about advertising!"

He exhaled heavily and leveled me with a look.

"How many birthday parties have you thrown for your children?" he asked.

"I don't know, one a year every year they've been alive."

"And other parties?"

"At least a dozen," I guessed.

"Then you're perfectly qualified for the job." He tapped his knuckles on the counter and then turned to Sophie. "Let's get going, Squirt." She turned and waved at me as he opened the door and let in a rush of cold Idaho air.

"See you tomorrow at eight-thirty," he called over his shoulder.

<u>Five</u>
Jackson

I waited on pins and needles for Emily to show up, hoping she didn't let me down by declining my job offer. It wasn't like I'd actually gotten her to accept it to begin with. I sort of just pushed it on her and decided that she would give up everything else and come work for me. It was crazy, just like she'd said.

By nine, Bea walked into my office with a very nervous-looking Emily behind her. She knocked twice on the door before stepping inside.

"Good morning, Jackson," she said, holding her hands in front of her. "We've finished Emily's paperwork, but I wasn't sure where you wanted me to have her set up."

I looked around my office and then pointed at the conference table in the corner.

"Go ahead and set her up over there, and I'll be right with her."

"You don't want her at Justine's desk?" Bea questioned.

"No. I've spoken with Denny's assistant, and she's agreed to handle the phones and scheduling for both of us right now, so I'm going to have Emily start on the holiday tasks."

She nodded and then left us, closing the door behind us.

"I'll be there in just a minute," I said as I finished the email I'd been working on.

Emily lingered in the corner of the room and set her purse on the table but didn't bother to sit down. It was different to see her in this element compared to how she was at the salon. I pressed send, then stood up and crossed the room to where she was standing.

"Have a seat," I offered, pulling out a plush rolling chair before taking the one across from her.

She tucked her skirt beneath her, then slid her chair to the table and placed her hands in front of her.

"How are you feeling?" I asked, guilt washing over me for making her nervous and uncomfortable.

"I'm okay," she replied quietly. "It's a lot to take in."

I nodded and leaned back in the chair to give her more space.

"You didn't tell me you *owned* the company," she blurted out.

"I didn't know it was of importance."

"It's not, I guess. I just feel like you're a totally different person than the kind uncle who's been bringing his niece in to get her hair done." She laughed, but I could hear the uneasiness in it.

"I'm still the same guy; I just happen to run a successful business in addition to taking care of Sophie."

"I can see that." She looked around the large office, taking in the ornate decorations on the wall and dark cherry wood furniture.

"So, where do you want me to start?" she asked, finally letting her shoulders fall as she looked up at me.

"We have two large functions that I need your help planning," I explained. "The first is the company holiday party. Justine, my former assistant, had started looking into venues for it, but nothing was ever confirmed. So, we're starting from scratch because most places are already booked."

I slid a notepad and pen over to her, and she started taking notes.

"How many people will be attending?" she questioned with her hand hovering above the paper. "And is it employees only, employees and spouses, or are you doing a family-friendly event?"

"It's employees and significant others. Probably fifty people, max. Back in New York, we'd do a fancy dinner and drinks, but this is the first time I've hosted one in Sugarplum Falls, so I'm not sure what our options are. Justine didn't give me much insight into what she'd found other than the names of places that are no longer available."

"Okay. Do you want to stick with the fancy party this year, or do you want to mix it up?"

"What do you think? You seem to know the town better than me; what are people more interested in?"

She leaned back in her seat and tapped the pen.

"Honestly, I'm not sure I've been here long enough to know either, but it depends on what tone you want to send to your staff here. They're all still getting to know you, just like you're getting to know them. Is the New York office doing a fancy party this year too?"

I nodded.

"Well then, I say do the same. If you want both branches to be equal, it wouldn't be fair to do an expensive party for those in New York and then only do something small for those in Sugarplum Falls. Plus, this would be a great way to start if you want to build camaraderie between the two branches."

"Okay, fair enough. Let's move forward with a nice dinner and drinks. Please look into some hotels close by and see if they have ballrooms we can rent. Also, please check into discounted room blocks if anyone wants to spend the night."

She nodded and took down the notes I'd given her. Once she was done, I dove into the bigger project that would probably be the thing that would send her packing her bags and bursting through the door to get away.

"The second item I need you to handle is the Sugarplum Falls Frosty Fest." I attempted to grin but noticed the way she pulled back hesitantly when I said it.

"We're hosting a booth, and apparently, nothing has been set up. I have zero ideas what to do, so I'm passing the baton to you." I extended my hands out in front of me.

"You're so kind," she replied sarcastically, narrowing her eyes playfully at me. "But don't worry, my friend is actually on the planning committee for the event, so I'll check in with her and see what's already being done. Last I knew, they already had people signed up for the giving tree and reindeer kisses, but I'm sure there are games or food stuff we can help with. I'll come up with a list of ideas once I know more. When do you need both of these by?"

I grimaced and pulled my lips into a thin line before responding.

"Friday."

She dropped the pen she was holding and stared at me.

"As in *two days*?!"

I inhaled slowly and then blew it out.

"I told you I needed help."

She shook her head and then smiled.

"And I knew you were crazy, yet here I am."

BLAME IT ON THE MISTLETOE

<u>Six</u>
Emily

The first few hours flew by in a breeze as I took notes and made phone calls to secure a venue for the company holiday party. In between calls, I'd worked on a list of ideas for the booth that Mason, Inc. would be hosting at the festival and reached out to my friend Jasmin for an update on what they still needed.

Jackson sat at his desk, focused with a scowl on his face the majority of the morning. By eleven, I needed to stretch my legs, so I got up and went to the breakroom that Bea had shown me earlier during the tour she'd given me.

An empty coffee pot was left on the burner, so I cleaned it out to start a fresh pot. I wasn't sure if Jackson was a coffee drinker or how he took his coffee if so, but the least I could do was make sure there was a fresh pot if he wanted some.

I was searching for filters when I heard someone come in. My back was turned toward the door as I tried to balance on a chair while I reached to the back of the cabinet, trying to grab the package I had spotted.

"Need a hand?" Jackson asked, his voice deeper than I remembered.

I spun around, startled, and knocked the filters straight at his head. He ducked and then reached out a hand to hold me steady as I wobbled from the sudden movement.

"Sorry," I laughed, accepting his help as he guided me down from the chair.

"You know, you could've asked for help, and I would've grabbed them for you."

"I didn't want to bother you. I know you're busy."

"I'm never too busy to help, Emily."

I lowered my head and tucked a strand of hair behind my ear.

He bent down and picked up the bag of filters, then set them on the counter next to the coffee maker.

"Need a pick me up?" he asked, nodding to the supplies I'd gotten ready.

"Yeah, it was a late night, and I'm starting to drag. I thought I'd see if you wanted a cup too."

He searched my face for a moment but didn't say anything.

"How about I make the coffee, and you make the popcorn?" he offered, reaching into a cabinet and pulling down a jar of kernels.

I raised my brow and smiled.

"Popcorn?"

"I like to snack," he said with a shrug.

"You keep surprising me." I laughed and took the jar while he worked on starting a pot of coffee.

I felt a sense of nostalgia wash over me as I added the kernels to the popcorn maker, remembering the one my grandparents had when I was a little girl. I loved sitting in front of it, watching as the popcorn danced across the glass.

I inhaled deeply, taking in the heavenly coffee aroma as Jackson filled two oversized mugs for us. Once the popcorn was ready, I grabbed some napkins and followed him back to the office.

We sat down at the conference table with the bowl in between us.

"So," he started as he popped a piece of popcorn into his mouth. "How are things going so far?"

I wiped my mouth and finished chewing the bite I'd just taken, then reached over and grabbed the notepad I had written my notes on.

"Not good," I mumbled, looking over the list that I'd made. Almost every place was crossed off because it was no longer available.

His brows pulled together, and I noticed the concern wash over his face.

"Unfortunately, all of the hotels in town are already booked for different events. I've checked to see if there are any businesses close by that we could make work, but everything is either too small or already committed to something."

He exhaled heavily and rubbed his temples with his fingers.

"Okay, what about restaurants? Could we possibly rent a private room somewhere?"

I shook my head and pulled my lips into a thin line.

"There aren't that many restaurants in town that can do what you're looking for. Sugarplum Falls doesn't have many upscale options for dining. Unless you want to have everyone travel to the next town over, you're not going to find much as far as something big enough to host employees and significant others."

"So, what are the options? Not do anything at all?" He scrubbed a hand down his face and tossed a piece of popcorn into his mouth. "I'm not making a great impression with Sugarplum Falls, am I?"

I pursed my lips and tried to think outside the box. I'd spent the morning waiting for people to call me back after checking to see if they could pull any strings to make something work for us. I had a feeling it was going to be hard, but I hadn't expected it to be impossible.

"What if I just give everyone large holiday bonuses to make up for not having a company party?"

I shook my head and frowned. That definitely wouldn't go over well if the employees in New York found out that the ones in Sugarplum Falls got a bonus they didn't. Sure, people enjoyed a free meal and open bar, but cash always ruled everything.

"Why not just do it here?" I asked, suddenly having a perfect idea.

"What?" He pulled his head back and looked at me like I was crazy.

"I'm serious," I laughed. "There's plenty of room, and you could have it catered."

"Where would we put everyone?"

I remembered the large open area that Bea led me through this morning before heading back to the offices. It was beautiful, with tiled marble floors and full-length windows that curved inward, creating the perfect space to set up a buffet.

"You could use the conference room. If we move the big table and chairs out, there's plenty of room to set up some six-foot tables and folding chairs. We can decorate and make it feel warm and cozy."

"But what about the food? There's not enough space for that and places for people to sit."

"No," I agreed, feeling excited as I saw it all coming together in my head. "But we can use the space across from the reception desk for the food. We can put up a few trees in front of the windows, then maybe three or four tables set up with food and drinks. It can be buffet-style. And if you still want to have an open bar, we can look at what we need to do to set it up, but we could use the reception desk as a bar. We already have a breakroom that we can let the caterer use to prepare and store everything. And everyone has an office, so they can store coats and purses in there. Once dinner is over, we can clear the tables out and convert the conference room into a dance floor."

He grabbed a handful of popcorn and ate it as he thought about what I was saying.

I tapped my pen anxiously, waiting for his response.

"So," I prodded. "What do you think?"

He tossed the last piece in his mouth and chewed.

"I think we can make it work. I'd rather do something here than not do anything at all."

"Yes!" I squealed excitedly.

"But there's still one problem," he said evenly. "We don't have a caterer. And I'm guessing that it's going to be hard finding one with such late notice."

I grabbed my phone from the table and started texting. I could feel his eyes on me as I waited for a response.

"I have someone who can do it," I announced, holding my phone to show him.

"You just happen to know a caterer who isn't booked two weeks before Christmas?"

"I do." I grinned, feeling like I was sitting on top of the world. "My friend, Carmen, is one of the *best* cooks I've ever met, and she's looking to start her own catering business."

"So she hasn't done this before?"

"No," I said gently. "But everyone has to start somewhere. Plus, you need her as much as she needs you."

He arched a brow, and I could see the battle raging inside of whether or not to allow this to happen or to pull the plug on it.

"Fine, you're right," he sighed, dropping his hand heavily on the table. "Have her put together a few menu options for the night, and I'll review it for approval before Friday."

"Okay, perfect. Did you decide on when you wanted to have the party?"

He looked at me again like I was crazy, and I tried to stifle my giggle. He was kinda cute when he was stressed.

"No, I assumed that Justine had taken care of that."

He picked up his phone and flicked his thumb as he scrolled

through something on his screen.

"Shit," he muttered under his breath.

"What's wrong?"

He looked up and locked eyes with me.

"She scheduled it and sent out the invite to the employees already."

"Okay, great," I said, trying to be enthusiastic about it. "When is it?"

"Saturday."

I leaned back against the chair and felt the air whoosh out of me. That left us two days to plan, decorate, and coordinate everything for the party while also getting the girls ready for the pageant that afternoon. Suddenly, things in Sugarplum Falls didn't seem so sweet.

<u>Seven</u>
Jackson

If I thought I was busy, I hadn't seen anything until I witnessed Emily in action. Once we had the general plan outlined for the holiday party, she went full force with getting everything set up. She made phone calls and secured everything we needed, from renting tables and chairs to booking a company to handle the open bar. It was amazing to watch her work, but it also put me behind on what I needed to get done.

I checked in with Sunny several times to see how Sophie was doing and was pleasantly surprised to hear that she'd had a better day at school and that they were working on Christmas decorations at home. Sunny was young, maybe early twenties, but was the best nanny—hands down. She was patient with Sophie, and I found them laughing together so often that I wondered what the secret was that she used to bring that side of Sophie out. I seemed to constantly struggle with it lately.

By four o'clock, my head was throbbing, but I knew there was still too much to get done, so there was no stopping. Emily was sitting across the office from me, typing something on the laptop when I heard my email notification ding. I looked down to find a new email from her.

A smile tugged at my lips as I opened it and found an evite for the holiday party. Inside the body of the email, she asked that I review it before she sent it out to the rest of the staff. While they had already been notified that the holiday party was scheduled for this Saturday per the email Justine had sent, they didn't have any details about it, which would make it hard for parents to plan around their children and find a babysitter at the last minute.

I forced the smile off of my face and clicked the reply button.

It was silly to be this formal with her, especially when she was sitting right across from me. But I also enjoyed the idea of this forbidden office romance that had been dancing through my head all afternoon and wanted to entertain the fantasy for a few more minutes. I knew there was probably nothing there, and it was likely all one-sided, but I couldn't shake the way I felt around Emily.

I pressed send and watched as she leaned forward to see the screen, then moved her finger over the mousepad on the laptop to open it.

Her lips turned up into a small smile as she tilted her head and replied to my request to have her send it out ASAP.

An email arrived a few seconds later with a simple *yes, sir*, stirring something deeper inside that I needed to shut off immediately. Now wasn't the time or place to start entertaining *those* kinds of thoughts.

I pushed away from my desk abruptly as if the email was somehow going to burn me. She looked over as I startled her.

"How are things going with the planning?" I asked dumbly, given that I already knew from eavesdropping on her the entire afternoon.

"Good, I have the caterer set up, the chairs and tables will be delivered tomorrow before noon, and the bar service will come set up by four o'clock on Saturday. Appetizers will start around five when guests start arriving, and then dinner will be served at six."

"Sounds like you've got it all taken care of. Thank you."

"Don't thank me yet," she laughed. "I still need to get decorations and put everything together."

"Can't I hire someone to do that stuff?"

"You can," she shrugged. "But why pay for something that I can do myself?"

Now it was my turn to shrug. I was so used to having everything that I needed handled for me without any second thoughts. Money had never been an issue, but I was quickly learning that it didn't make as much of a difference in Sugarplum Falls.

"I can easily afford to hire someone to come in and decorate for us, Emily," I said softly. "That's not part of your job description, nor would I like for you to spend your time focused on that. We still need to come up with a plan for the booth at the festival."

She stood up, grabbed her coat from the rack in the corner, and put it on.

"I hate to break it to you, boss, but you're not going to find someone who can come decorate for you on such short notice."

"Why not? Everyone in Sugarplum Falls loves decorating for the holidays. Surely there's someone I can hire to do it for me."

She shook her head.

"I've reached out to everyone I know. Between preparing for the holiday pageant this weekend and the festival, everyone is tied up and busy. It won't take me long to get the stuff we need."

"Fine," I exhaled. "But I'll go with you. I don't want you trying to carry everything on your own, nor do I want you paying for any of it."

"Okay, sounds great."

She looked down at her watch and frowned.

"What's wrong?"

"Nothing; I didn't realize how late it was getting."

"We don't have to do this today. If you tell me what you want, I can run out and grab it. I'll probably be working late tonight anyway."

"What about Sophie?"

"She's with her nanny."

"But won't she be upset if she doesn't see you tonight?" She tilted her head to the side and studied me.

I hadn't thought about what the impact of my working late tonight would be on Sophie. It wasn't unusual for me to work late, but I hadn't had to since Sophie came to live with me. This would be new and another disruption in her little world.

"Fuck, I hadn't thought about that."

"I need to stop by Wally's before five, but after that, we can go grab the decorations and come back here. What if we make it a family event, and you have your nanny bring Sophie here? I'll have my mom bring the girls, and we can knock the decorations out tonight."

"Do you really think that'll work?"

"Absolutely. My girls always get bored at home, and they *love* decorating. Plus, they can help watch Sophie. My youngest is around her age, so I'm sure they'll enjoy playing while everyone else works," she laughed.

"Okay, let's do it."

She smiled and texted her mom while I called Sunny to let her know about the change in plans.

Two hours later, we stumbled back into the office with arms full of shopping bags and a few guys following us with the larger items we had picked up. I'd never spent that much money in such a short period of time, but I had meant it when I told Emily that cost was of zero importance as she shopped for the decorations.

Sunny dropped Sophie off shortly after Emily's mom, Megan, brought Penelope and Gracelyn. The girls looked just like their mom, and I could tell their family had strong genetics when I noticed how much Emily looked like her mom.

I took the liberty of ordering a few pizzas, and we had dinner in the conference room before we moved the furniture out. It was amazing how much bigger the room felt after the large oak table was moved into an empty office and the oversized office chairs were removed. Emily was right; this room was plenty big to accommodate everyone on Saturday without feeling cramped.

"So, where do we start?" I asked after we finished eating and cleaned up the mess.

Sophie was busy playing with Gracelyn, Emily's youngest, while Penelope played on her phone. Emily gave her a look that earned her an eye roll before she tucked it in her pocket and folded her arms across her chest. I cringed when I thought about Sophie having that kind of attitude with me when she got older.

"I think we should start in the waiting area and set up the trees."

I felt a warm blush flush across my face, embarrassed to admit that I had no idea how to decorate a Christmas tree. It was another one of those things that were just done for me.

Emily licked her lips but kept from laughing when she noticed my discomfort.

"Actually, I think my mom and I can handle the trees with the girls if you want to take care of hanging the lights?"

I pictured myself standing on a ladder with a nail gun, looking manlier than shit. I raised a brow approvingly.

"Sounds like a plan," I said, my voice a little deeper than needed.

"Alright, I'll check in here in a little bit. Just holler if you need help."

I nodded and headed back to my office to grab my phone before we got started. As I was heading back to the conference room, I passed by Emily as she bent over to unpack the box the artificial tree came in. Her skirt stretched tightly across her ass, making me instantly hard. I adjusted myself as discreetly as possible, then rushed into the conference room, ignoring the way her mom was smirking when she caught me checking her daughter out.

Eight
Emily

The evening passed quickly with everyone bustling around, getting the office decorated. I was proud that my girls jumped in to help with little prodding but even more so that they took Sophie under their wing, making sure she wasn't left out.

We decorated the three trees in no time while Jackson grunted and cursed as he hung the lights in the conference room. I was surprised by how much he'd gotten done, given that he'd struggled so much in the beginning. When Jackson said he was used to paying people to do things for him, I thought he was exaggerating. Tonight proved he was telling the truth, and I found myself laughing more than I should have.

"I'm going to go ahead and take the girls home," my mom said, standing beside me as we admired how beautiful the waiting area looked with the soft lights hanging above the trees and the rose gold decorations that adorned each one.

"Okay, thank you."

It was already after nine and well past their bedtime. She went to gather their stuff while I checked in on Jackson.

The conference room had come together nicely, and he was adding the final strand of garland when I walked in.

"It looks great," I said, smiling as I took in the room's ambiance.

"It doesn't even look like the same room," he laughed, running a hand through his hair.

His sleeves were rolled up to his elbows, showing off a tattoo on his forearm that I hadn't seen before.

"My mom is going to take the girls home. I can stay and help you finish if you want?"

He stepped down from the ladder and looked at Sophie lying down on a pile of coats in the corner. My girls had made a bed for her earlier when she started yawning.

"I'm going to call it a night too. Need to get that one in bed before it gets too late."

"Want help packing stuff up?"

"Nah, I've got it, but thank you."

I ran my hands down my skirt, smoothing it down even though it didn't need it. I was suddenly feeling nervous around Jackson again, and I couldn't figure out why. It was like I was stalling having to leave, even though I had spent the entire day with him and would see him in the morning.

"Okay, well, I guess I'll see you in the morning," I stammered, trying to smile, so he didn't notice how weird I was acting.

"Sounds good, have a good night. Thank you for all of your help today. I couldn't have done any of this without you." He looked around the room and beamed proudly.

"No problem."

I turned and left the room, taking my nerves with me.

My mom already had the girls packed up when I joined

them in the hallway outside of the office.

"Alright, let's get home," I said, smiling at my two sleepy girls.

Once we got to the house, the girls went in and got ready for bed while my mom and I sat down in the living room. It was a long day, and I hadn't realized how tired I was.

"Thank you for all of your help tonight," I said, catching her eye. "I know Jackson appreciates it as well."

"My pleasure. It's what we do, helping each other when they need it."

I smiled and leaned back against the couch. She was right, though; we always stepped in and helped if someone needed it. That was how I was raised, and it was how I was also bringing my girls up.

"He's nice," she commented, her eyes lighting up when she spoke.

"Yeah, he is."

I didn't say anything more, nor did I have to. I knew where she was going with the conversation, but I wasn't ready to have it.

"Sophie is just the cutest little thing, too," she added. "Such a sweet girl."

I nodded and smiled. It was fun to see her laughing and playing with my girls. For a moment, I stopped and thought about what it might look like if they were part of our family. That wasn't something I had expected, and I struggled with how comfortable I felt with it, given that Mark still held such a huge spot in my heart.

"She's a darling girl," I agreed before getting up and stretching. "I'm going to go say goodnight to the girls. You sticking around for a bit?"

"No, I think I'll head home and call it a night as well. I'll pick the girls up from school tomorrow and take them to my house so they can work on finishing their projects."

"Okay, sounds good. Thanks again for tonight."

"No problem. Get some rest." She smiled and leaned in to kiss my cheek before leaving.

I locked the door after her and then went to Gracelyn's room. She was already in bed with the covers pulled up to her ears and snoring softly. I leaned down and gently kissed the top of her head.

I had expected Penelope to be asleep already as well, but I was surprised to find her sitting in her bed looking through a photo album I gave her last year for Christmas. I felt my heart tighten, knowing how hard the holidays were going to be for them this year, not having their dad to celebrate with. Last year had been rough with Mark going through chemo and radiation, but nothing like what it would be this year.

"Whatcha got there, Pumpkin?"

"It's the family photos we did right before daddy got sick."

She pulled the picture out from the plastic covering and handed it to me. It was my favorite picture of us, taken the summer before he was diagnosed with cancer.

"I remember this day," I said softly, sitting pretzel-style on her bed, facing her.

"We had spent the day driving up the coast and then stopped to pick strawberries in the field. Do you remember that giant bumblebee that kept dive bombing your dad's head?"

She laughed and nodded. The smile on her face quickly turned to sadness as tears washed over her face. I reached over and pulled her into my arms, hugging her as tight as I could without hurting her.

"It's okay to cry and be sad, my love," I whispered.

"I miss him so much," she cried.

"Me too, baby. Me too."

My heart shattered into a million pieces every time I saw the girls struggle with the loss. I wiped my tears away with the back of my hand and continued to hold my sweet girl as she crumbled beneath the weight of her tears.

Soon, her breathing calmed, and I knew that she was exhausted. I felt her pull away and gave her one last squeeze before helping her put the photo back in the album and setting it on her nightstand.

She crawled beneath the blankets and let me cover her. I wanted to crawl beside her and hug the sadness away, but I knew she needed her rest as much as I did.

Within a few minutes, I could hear the soft sounds of her breathing as she drifted to sleep.

I kissed her goodnight and then headed to my bedroom. Once I was alone, I sat on the bed and held my head in my hands as I cried. It had been awhile since I'd allowed myself to feel the pain of losing Mark, but tonight I couldn't stop it if I tried.

BLAME IT ON THE MISTLETOE

<u>Nine</u>

Jackson

When I got to the office Thursday morning, I couldn't believe how different everything looked. The office had been completely transformed, and I felt like I had stepped foot in one of those Hallmark movies. It was magical, and the mood seemed to shift as the employees started filing in for the day.

I heard the whispered oohs and ahhs as people walked around, taking in the decorations. I felt bad that I hadn't bothered to decorate the office, and even worse, I hadn't thought about how much it would impact the employees' morale if I did. After all, Sugarplum Falls loved Christmas, so it was stupid not to consider that they would also want to be surrounded by the merriment at work.

I glanced at the clock on the wall, knowing that Emily would be coming in any minute. I tried to pretend like I wasn't sitting there waiting for her, so I kept my attention turned toward my emails, forcing myself to get started on my day.

I confirmed the delivery of the tables and chairs, as well as some extra decorations that Emily suggested last night. I placed an order online after I got Sophie home, and thankfully, they had everything in stock and available for pick up today. I was still waiting for the email with the menu options from Emily's friend that agreed to cater the event for us and needed to look over the paperwork for the bar service. There was a lot to do in a short amount of time, but I was beyond grateful for Emily's help with getting everything set up. I wanted to do something nice for her family to thank them for their help, but I had no idea what.

Back in New York, I could tell my assistant what I needed, and she would just handle it. If someone had a death in the family, she would take care of sending a card and a floral arrangement for the service, as well as taking care of having food delivered. If someone had a baby, she would put together a gift basket filled with whatever she thought they needed and have it delivered along with a hot meal. I didn't have to think about what to do or send; she just handled everything.

When I moved to Sugarplum Falls, she stayed in NY with her family, and I hadn't been able to find anyone to replace her. After five different assistants, I'd started to give up hope of finding anyone as capable as Jolene was until I saw Emily at work yesterday.

I was easily impressed with her when I first met her, and she was so kind to Sophie, but yesterday showed me a different side that I hadn't seen before. And if I was being completely honest with myself, I was more than intrigued and borderline obsessed with getting to know her more.

"Good morning," Emily said, breezing past me and leaving a light trail of perfume floating in the air behind her.

I looked up to see her walking past me to the conference table, wearing a tight-fitting red dress that pinched at her waist and then flowed out over her hips.

I swallowed hard and tried to force my eyes to look away, but the way her long legs looked in those skinny black heels made it impossible. She glanced at me over her shoulder as she took her coat off and pulled it down her arms.

"Morning," I managed to gruff out, clearing my throat.

"You okay?" she asked with a hint of a giggle.

"Yeah, my throat is just a little dry this morning. It must be hot in here."

You're making it hot in here.

I shifted under my desk and tried to turn my thoughts to anything that would lessen the stiffening in my briefs right now.

"Want me to turn on the fan?" she offered, bending over to pick up a pen that had fallen off the table.

I scrubbed a hand down my face and closed my eyes. She was going to be the death of me.

"I'm okay, thank you."

She smiled and sat down, sliding the chair forward so smoothly that it looked like she was floating. I must be hallucinating, high from a lack of sleep last night.

When I got home, I put Sophie in bed and then spent a few hours on the work I didn't get done yesterday. It was the end of the year, and we were busier than usual. It was great for business, but it sucked because I couldn't focus.

Ever since I met Emily last week, my thoughts were constantly on her, and it felt like nothing else—besides Sophie—mattered. I hated that she was getting so far under my skin, because this felt like an itch that I desperately wanted to scratch. The problem was that it wasn't that easy.

For one, I needed to stop and make sure Sophie was my

number one priority, which meant I didn't have time for a relationship. Second, Emily had just lost her husband not that long ago, and dating was probably the last thing on her mind. She likely just saw me as a friend, and I would be making a *huge* mistake if I were to take advantage of that. And the biggest issue was that she was now my employee, which meant she was off-limits.

I knew she would be the second the job offer came rolling off my tongue, but I didn't care. I even tried to convince myself that was why I'd offered her the job—to make it so I couldn't ask her out. But, I was so eager to see her again, that I threw out an offer I thought she couldn't turn down. Sure, I'd been selfish in that I wanted to spend time with her, and I really did need a new assistant, but deep down, I knew that Emily needed this job more than anything.

To cross that line and make a move on her would be wrong on so many levels, if only my stiff cock would get the message.

I spent the majority of the morning responding to emails and confirming more details for the holiday event. I still had no idea what Mason, Inc. was going to do for the Sugarplum Falls Frosty Fest, but I was counting on Emily to put something together as easily as she had for the company holiday party.

I was up to my eyeballs in reports scattered across my desk when Emily got up and grabbed something from the printer.

I tried to ignore how my body tingled as she got closer or how my heart raced when she accidentally placed her hand on mine when she set the papers beside me.

"Sorry," she said quietly. "I have the menu options you asked for. Let me know when you have time, and we can review them. I told Carmen that we would have an answer for her by two; that way, she has plenty of time to get the items she needs. Also, since this is last minute, we agreed that the menu options wouldn't be too extravagant. She'll add her touch, but it will be stuff that's easily accessible in large quantities."

"Okay," I said, pushing the other files to the side to make room for the report. "Did you want to go over it now?"

She glanced at her watch and frowned, then looked at the papers.

"Umm," she sighed. "Okay. Sure."

I pushed back in my chair and turned to the side to look at her. The way the light shined above her made her green eyes sparkle.

"I don't want to keep you from something," I said gently.

"No, it's okay. I'm here to work. That's what matters." She pulled her shoulders back and straightened her spine.

I studied her for a few minutes, knowing there was something going on that she wasn't telling me.

"Emily," I warned with a raised brow.

Instead of flinching or blushing like most women did around me, she arched hers and met my stare.

"It's nothing. Really."

I held my stance and continued to watch until she finally gave in.

"Fine," she sighed heavily. "I was trying to get to Waldon's before noon."

I looked down at the clock on my computer and saw that it was a little after 11:30.

"I won't be gone longer than the hour I get for lunch," she rushed to explain, suddenly pulling at the bottom of the cardigan she was wearing over her dress. "They're supposed to be getting their next shipment of toys in at noon, and I wanted to make sure I got there when they put them out, but I know it won't be right at noon, and if I'm a little late, I promise that I'll make up the hours. There's this doll that Gracelyn really wants, and I haven't been able to find it anywhere. They're not sure if they're getting one, but it's the *one thing* that she really, really wants and put it on her list to Santa, and if he can't deliver, then it will—"

"Okay," I laughed, holding up my hand and cutting her off.

"You don't have to worry about how long you're gone, Emily. It's fine."

"But there's a lot to get done, and I don't want to let you down."

I felt the words flying out of my mouth before I even thought them through.

"How about I go with you, and we can discuss the festival while we wait for them to put the new stock out? Then if needed, we can divide and conquer to get the doll."

"There's another toy I'm waiting for too. And some stuff for Penelope. And my mom." She scrunched her face.

"It's fine; I need to do some shopping myself. We can tackle several things at once."

I pushed away from my desk and hated the way I missed

the heat of her body as she moved back.

"Grab your stuff, I'll drive."

I turned and pulled the coat from the rack by the door, avoiding watching the way her body stretched as she slid into hers.

Fifteen minutes later, we were shivering in the cold, waiting at the end of the line of customers who were all there waiting for the same shipment Emily was.

I wondered if this was what I had sent my assistant into all those years of asking her to handle my shopping for me. It wasn't like I had many people to buy for—mainly my sister and Sophie, though, on occasion, I would have her shop for a girlfriend, but that was rare.

Finally, the line moved, and we inched our way inside. I could see the stress etched on Emily's face as she leaned on her tiptoes to see if the items she wanted were sitting on the shelves.

"So, what happens if they don't have the things you came here for?" I asked as I casually shoved my hands into my pockets.

"Then Christmas will be ruined, and I will have let my girls down," she said sadly with a smile, though I couldn't tell if she was joking or not.

"That's a lot of pressure for the holidays," I replied lightly, not having any clue what it actually felt like.

"Yeah, and it's harder with kids. Especially when they're still young enough to believe in Santa."

"Does Penelope still believe?"

She shook her head and then leaned to the side to see to the front of the line.

"No, a kid at school told her he wasn't real, and she came home crying. Mark decided that it was time to tell her the truth, so he sat down and explained it to her. But we made her agree that she wouldn't tell Gracelyn. She still believes."

I felt a hard knot form in my stomach, wondering what Sophie was expecting this year. Did she believe in Santa? Had some kid already ruined it for her? Did my sister do anything special with her during the holidays that I didn't know about? I hated that I spent so much of my life being busy and wrapped up in work that I didn't know these things about my family. They were all that I had left, but I knew nothing about them.

"Do you know what Sophie wants for Christmas?" Emily asked.

We stepped forward into the warmth of the store. There was still a solid line into the toy department and plenty of frustrated-looking parents storming out of the store. Emily's face dropped when she noticed them pass by empty-handed.

"I don't know," I admitted sheepishly. "I'm a terrible uncle, aren't I? I don't even know what my niece likes and haven't asked what she wants for Christmas."

She reached up and grabbed my arm with her gloved hand, searching my eyes before she spoke.

"You're not a terrible uncle, Jackson. You've only been doing this for a few weeks, and I can't imagine how life-changing this has been for you. Plus, you still have two weeks until Christmas; there's plenty of time."

I placed a hand over hers and gave it a gentle squeeze.

"Yeah, unless she asks for something that everyone else in here is fighting to get, and I can't find one."

She laughed and pulled me along with her as we moved forward.

The aisles were packed, but thankfully, I'd grabbed a shopping cart which gave us some space from everyone else. Emily moved quickly, putting items in the cart and then moving to the next thing on her lists. She had two, which she explained were wish lists from each child to Santa.

I guarded the basket with a little more force than necessary, but living in a big city made you expect the worst when it came to frantic shoppers who were fighting over a limited supply of something. I'd seen plenty of videos of people fighting over Black Friday sales, and I wasn't about to let anyone take the items Emily had worked so hard to get.

Finally, she grabbed the last item and smiled, relief washing over her as her shoulders relaxed.

"This is the last item," she said, adding the box of art supplies to the shopping cart.

"Alright, shall we head to the checkout?"

Her eyes bulged out of her head as if I'd just asked a ridiculous question—and maybe I had.

"No," she laughed. "Now I have to go through and sort everything. I'm not buying all of this."

"Why not?"

She tilted her head to the side, watching me in amazement.

"Because that's easily a couple hundred dollars worth of stuff."

I stayed quiet to keep from sounding stupid, but I really didn't understand what the problem was.

"I can't afford to buy all of this," she laughed, pointing to the stuff in the cart. "I grabbed it so I didn't miss out on it, but there's no way I can get everything. Now I'll go through and prioritize everything. I spend the same on each girl, but I also make sure I get them an even number of gifts, which can be hard given some of their stuff is more expensive than the rest."

My head felt like it was spinning. What she said made sense, but I couldn't imagine having to limit what I bought because of the cost. That had never been something I'd had to think about, yet it was a huge factor in what Emily bought for her children for Christmas.

I stepped back and watched as Emily organized the cart and separated items based on what she was getting for Penelope and what she was getting for Gracelyn. She tucked the lists for the girls into the top part of the shopping cart, and when she wasn't looking, I slid it into my coat pocket.

After she decided on the two toys to get for both girls, we headed to the checkout. She asked if I wanted to shop for Sophie while we were there, but I assured her that I would make an effort to see what she wanted first. I imagined I would just bring her to the store and let her go crazy picking out whatever she wanted, but then I remembered Emily and how her girls would only be getting a few toys and reconsidered.

While Emily was paying, I excused myself to take a phone call. I had business to take care of, but nothing that I wanted her to hear.

Ten
Emily

I had no idea what was keeping Jackson so long, but I was relieved that I had gotten the two gifts off of the girls' list that they had wanted the most. I knew that it was going to be hard coming up with enough things for them to open on Christmas day, as well as getting stuff from Santa, but I was determined to do the best I could.

I knew that the money I was making from Mason, Inc. would be more than enough to cover what I needed, but the problem was that Christmas was two weeks away, and I wouldn't get my first check until a few days before. If I waited until I got paid, everything would be sold out, and I would be even more screwed than I already felt.

Shoppers passed by me, muttering their frustrations over not getting what they came in for. It was a bit shocking to see so many disgruntled people in Sugarplum Falls, but being a parent, I understood where they were coming from. Nothing made you feel worse than not being able to deliver what your child asked for this time of year.

I rested against the cart by the front of the store while I waited for Jackson. My stomach growled loudly, drawing the attention of an elderly man passing by. I glanced at my watch and noticed that it was already after one. I felt bad for keeping Jackson away from the office for so long, especially if it meant he had to skip lunch today to get caught up.

"Sorry about that," he apologized, stuffing something into his pocket. "Are you ready to go?"

"I'm the one who should be apologizing. I didn't expect it to take this long. I'm sorry for tying up your day."

"It's not a problem."

He popped the trunk and loaded my bags before returning the cart to the corral. I smiled stupidly as I watched him work in his Armani suit, not bothered that he might get it dirty.

I climbed into the passenger seat and buckled up as he got in and started the car.

"Did you want to grab something to eat? We can do take out and eat in the office if that works for you?"

"Sure," I said nervously. It wasn't that I was afraid to share a meal with him, but every time he was physically around me, I felt these butterflies that rushed through me, making me feel like a teenage girl again.

As much as I enjoyed the rush of it, I also felt incredibly guilty for allowing myself to feel this way with another man. Mark hadn't been gone even a year yet, and I was already feeling attracted to someone else. It was too soon, and I knew it, so why didn't my body get the message?

"What are you in the mood for?" he asked, pulling me out of my thoughts and confusing me.

Had he been able to read my mind? Did he know I had been thinking about how it would feel if he touched me? Was he aware of the emotional turmoil that was bubbling inside me because of my desire for another man who wasn't my husband?

"I'm sorry?" My voice broke, giving me away.

"I asked what you wanted to eat," he said softly, rubbing his lips together. "But I'm very curious as to what you were thinking about when I asked."

My face flamed even hotter as a wave of embarrassment washed over me.

"I, um...." I couldn't get the words out if I tried.

He covered his mouth behind his fist and laughed as he looked out the window.

A few minutes later, he pulled into a parking lot with a handful of fast-food options. Well, technically, they were the only fast-food options.

"Alright," he said, rubbing his hands together and scanning the area. "You have your choice of Chinese, burgers, subs, or fried chicken. Anything sound good?"

"I'm not picky; whatever you pick is fine with me."

He turned in his seat and pinned me with a look.

"You may not be picky, but you should still have a say in what you eat. Believe it or not, I can go to several different places. Just tell me what you want, and I'll make it happen."

I felt my thighs involuntarily clench at his play on words—though I didn't imagine he did that on purpose.

"Um, I could really go for a burger and fries," I said awkwardly, shifting in my seat. It wasn't that I couldn't decide for myself; it was that I was constantly used to going off of whatever everyone else wanted. It started with Mark, and then I'd gotten so used to it that I always put the girls' wants and needs before my own.

"Sounds delicious," he agreed, pulling around to the drive-thru. "What do you want to drink?"

I rubbed my lips together as I leaned forward and looked at the menu. I'd been here a dozen times, but it felt different ordering for myself and no one else.

"I want a vanilla shake."

He raised his eyebrows and smiled, then leaned out of the window to order.

I tried to pay for our lunch, but he swatted my hand away and passed his credit card to the cashier before I could object. Plus, I was already flustered by the touch of his skin on mine and beating myself up once again for enjoying it.

I held the bags of food on my lap until we got back to the office, and Jackson helped me carry it inside. I had already forgotten about my bags until Jackson ran down to the car to get them while I finished clearing the conference table, so we had a place to eat.

When he returned, I thanked him for grabbing my stuff and tucked it into the corner, so it was out of the way.

"The food smells delicious; good choice," he said as he took off his jacket and sat down.

You smell delicious.

I tried to ignore the cedar scent that filled the air around me as he reached across the table to grab the file we had been working on. I'd already brought the menu options from this morning over so we could discuss those and finalize a decision before it was too late.

"Thank you again for lunch." I took a small bite of my cheeseburger, trying to remain as ladylike as possible as I ate. I was starving and the temptation to shove the food in my mouth and devour it within minutes was a bit overwhelming.

"Here are the menu options," I said after I finished chewing. "We need to get an answer to Carmen soon."

I slid the papers in front of him and watched as his eyes roamed across the page, looking over each option.

"What do you think we should go with?" He lifted his straw to his lips and sucked some of the milkshake through.

I quickly looked away and scolded myself for another inappropriate thought. He was my boss, for goodness sake. And I was still grieving my husband. What in the world had gotten into me?

Not Jackson, that's for sure.

"Umm, I don't know." I shook my head and leaned forward to look at the papers, needing more of a distraction even though I knew what the menus consisted of. "I don't know the employees well enough to know what they'd like."

He leaned back in his chair and pushed a french fry into his mouth.

"I don't know them that well either, unfortunately."

"Well, what do you usually do in New York?"

"My assistant used to handle it," he said with a tight smile.

I nodded and sighed heavily. He hired me for a reason, and that was to help him make these sorts of decisions.

"Okay, well, if it were me, I would go with at least one

vegetarian option. That way, you're covered in case any of the employees or their significant others don't eat meat. Then, I would do the chicken and steak options. You could do the lobster tail, but I have a feeling that will get rather expensive, and you don't know if anyone has a shellfish allergy."

I felt his gaze on me as I spoke, sending goosebumps over my skin.

"Done. Please let Carmen know that we'll do the three different options exactly as she has them listed on the menu. Also, if you can, please generate an email to the staff asking them to select a dinner option for themselves and their guest. I know it's short notice but request that they submit it by five today at the latest. I'll confirm the totals via email to Carmen by six."

I scribbled the information on my notepad and debated whether to send the email now, so people had more time to decide.

"It can wait until after you eat," he assured me as if reading my mind. "I'll also bump the numbers up across the board. Anything that's left over will be offered to the staff that night and then donated to the shelter, so it doesn't go to waste."

"Sounds great," I said happily, setting my pen down and picking up my burger. "So, have you finished the rest of your Christmas shopping, aside from Sophie?"

He chewed his bite and then wiped his face with a napkin.

"I don't really have anyone else to shop for. My sister, Cammy, was the only family I had left besides Sophie."

I frowned, and he laughed.

"I know, it's pathetic. But I've been busy with work and

never bothered to keep in touch with anyone."

"Don't you have a best friend or colleagues that you're close to?" I felt stupid for asking, but it made me so sad that he didn't have anyone in his life other than his niece.

"I was a big party animal in college but quickly grew out of that. I started my own business at twenty-four and haven't looked back. Success required my full attention, and I didn't have time for the nonsense that came with forcing a relationship to work."

"Wow," I said quietly.

"I know, I know. It's not the first time I've been accused of being a coldhearted workaholic. But honestly, this is what makes me happy. I'd like to think that I would be married and settled down by now if I met the right person along the way, but it just never happened."

I finished my food and then washed it down with a drink.

"I met Mark when I turned thirty. I knew in an instant that he was my forever. Everything about him was perfection, and things moved so quickly for us. We moved in together and got married, all within six months of meeting each other. I got pregnant with Penelope right away, then four years later, I had Gracelyn. I thought we were getting our happily ever after, but cancer had different plans for us."

My chest tightened as the words poured out of me. It had been a long time since I'd talked to anyone about Mark, let alone someone who didn't already know our history.

"I'm so sorry, Emily. I can't imagine what it's been like for you and the girls."

"Thank you," I whispered, trying to blink away the tears. "I guess my point for telling you that was to assure you that it's never too late to find that. I didn't think that I would wait until I was thirty before starting my family, and I sure as hell didn't think I would be starting over at forty."

It was awkwardly quiet after that, and I desperately wished I could disappear.

Jackson got up and threw away our trash, and I was relieved that he was just brushing past it.

Then he came back, sat down, and placed his hands in front of him on the table.

"I can't begin to understand what you've lost, Emily, but I can tell you that even though you might feel like you're stumbling as you try to get back on your feet, you're one of the strongest people that I've ever met. I've seen how much my sister struggled, being a single mom to Sophie. You remind me so much of Cammy, it's crazy. But you're doing just fine, Emily. You and your girls will find your way, and I know that happiness lies in your future."

No matter how hard I tried, I couldn't keep the tears in as they rushed out and trickled down my cheeks. I covered my face with my hands, attempting to keep him from seeing what his words had done to me.

Suddenly, my chair was spun around, and strong arms were lifting me to a standing position.

Refusing to let him see me this way, I kept my hands over my face and felt his body as it pressed against mine in a warm embrace.

It had been so long since anyone hugged me this way that

I felt myself losing the battle I'd been fighting all along. I wanted to feel this way again—safe, cared for, and wanted.

But Jackson wasn't touching me in a way that was sexual—that was the weird thing. I craved this so much, and it wasn't even because it had been so long since I'd had sex. It was because it had been so long since a man had held me without wanting anything in return. Mark used to do this, but once he got sick, he wasn't strong enough to hold himself up, let alone me.

For a few moments, I allowed myself to relish in the comfort of his embrace and not worry about anything else.

<u>Eleven</u>
Jackson

Friday flew by in a blur with people rushing around, setting up for Saturday's holiday party. I'd been stressed with trying to oversee everything and get the contracts done that were due any day now, but I couldn't stop thinking about Emily.

The way she felt in my arms was unlike anything that I'd experienced before. I didn't want to let go, even though I knew it was wrong. Not only was she my employee, but she was also crying because she was still grieving her husband and his tragic, untimely death.

We'd tried to focus and get work done, but I knew she was just as distracted as I was. I wondered if it was because she had also felt something when I held her. I didn't want to get my hopes up that she had, but part of me was convinced that there was something there, simmering beneath the surface that neither of us was ready to acknowledge.

Saturday was supposed to be a relaxing day, but I severely misunderstood how much stress went into a kid's pageant. I was supposed to have Sophie to Emily's house by eleven so she could do her hair, but instead, we were digging through stuff in her bedroom, trying to find a pink stuffed bunny.

I called Emily and let her know that we weren't going to make it. I knew that she could hear the frustration in my tone and knew that something was wrong. When I explained about the missing Mr. Flopsy, she confirmed that she and the girls were on their way over. I gave her my address and waited impatiently for them to get there.

I was in the kitchen, pouring another cup of coffee, when I heard the doorbell.

Sophie had given up finding the bunny and had locked herself in her room, refusing to let me in. I'd never felt like a bigger failure in my life until now.

"Hey, sorry," I apologized as I pulled the door open and stepped to the side to let them in.

The girls came in first, wiping their shoes on the mat before they shuffled to the side and waited for direction from Emily.

"It's not a problem," Emily assured me and pulled her jacket off before hanging it on the coat rack by the door. She nodded to the girls, and they did the same. "Did you find the bunny?"

I shook my head and ran a hand through my hair.

"Okay, no worries. We'll find it together. Where's Sophie?"

"In her room. She locked me out. Said that she hated me and wanted her mom."

The words pierced my heart like a knife, the same way they had when she spoke them.

Emily squeezed my arm and smiled sympathetically.

"She doesn't mean it," she whispered, then looked at her girls. "You'll find that they say a lot of stuff they don't mean. Mind if I try to talk to her?"

I sighed heavily and extended my hand in the direction of her room.

"Be my guest."

She nodded and then looked at her girls.

"I need a few minutes alone with Sophie, but I'd like it if you both could help Jackson try to find her stuffed animal. Okay?"

They both agreed, and she walked quietly down the hall and knocked on Sophie's door.

"Hey, Sophie. It's Emily. Can I come in?"

I couldn't hear what she said, but Emily smiled softly over her shoulder before she opened the door and closed it behind her.

Thirty minutes later, the girls and I still hadn't found Mr. Flopsy. Sophie's door opened, and Emily came out holding her hand as she clung to her side. Her face was red and splotchy from crying.

I wanted to hold her and make it all go away, but I knew I couldn't. I wouldn't understand the pain of that kind of loss the way she did. Or the way Emily did. I felt like an outsider, lost and unsure of what to do.

Suddenly Sophie looked up at me, and tears filled her eyes again. I knelt down and opened my arms, relieved when she came running over and let me hold her.

My heart wanted to explode with love for this little girl.

"I'm sorry I said mean things," she cried. "I was really sad and mad that I couldn't find Mr. Flopsy."

"It's okay sweet girl. Don't you ever worry about that." I squeezed her tighter, then pulled back so I could see her face. "I'm sorry that we lost Mr. Flopsy. I know how much he means to you."

"Actually," Emily said, stepping forward and holding her hands out to Sophie. "Gracelyn found this guy in the kitchen, under the table. Is this Mr. Flopsy?"

Sophie spun around and gasped before reaching out and taking the bunny from Emily. She held it close to her chest and closed her eyes as she squeezed it.

"Mr. Flopsy!" she squealed, then started crying again. "Thank you for finding him." She smiled at Gracelyn, who was hugging her mom and smiling back.

"Alright, now that we've found the elusive bunny, we better get started on your girls' hair before the pageant starts." Emily clapped her hands, and the girls all giggled.

I sat on the sidelines, handing Emily brushes and combs and random things from the bag she brought with her, having no idea how to help her. I watched as her fingers moved quickly, pulling strands of hair here and there until it was this beautiful hairdo for each of the girls.

Gracelyn and Penelope brought their outfits to change into at the house and helped Sophie get into hers. I'd never been to a holiday pageant before and didn't know what to expect, but when Sophie came out dressed like an angel with Gracelyn, I felt another stabbing pain in my heart. The amount of love I felt for my niece was getting overwhelming by the day, and I worried that my heart might soon explode at this rate.

"You girls look beautiful," I said, smiling at the three of them together.

"You sure do," Emily agreed. "Now, let's get going before we're late."

She ushered the kids outside and loaded them into the car while I locked up.

Once we got to the school, the parking lot was already full. I looked at the clock on the dashboard and knew that the girls would be late if I didn't drop them off. Emily and I had agreed to carpool, which seemed to work out for the best.

"Do you want to take the girls inside while I find parking?" I asked, pulling up to the curb in front of the gymnasium.

"That's a good idea. I'll save you a seat."

I nodded and pressed the button to unlock the doors while Emily helped them out. Once they were inside, I pulled around and searched for a parking spot.

By the time I got inside, the lights were already dimming, and the pageant was about to start. I caught sight of Emily as she waved me over, scooting next to her mom to free the seat she'd saved for me.

I sat down, smiled at her, and then turned my attention to the stage.

The curtain pulled back, and I immediately searched the group of kids wearing the same angel costume until I found Sophie. She was next to Gracelyn, both of them holding hands while they started singing with the other kids.

I glanced at Emily and found her covering her mouth as she smiled, seeing the same thing I did.

I wanted to reach down and hold her hand but didn't. I wanted to comment about how cute *our kids* looked together but didn't. I wanted to do so many things with Emily that I couldn't allow myself to do, and it was frustrating.

The kids continued to sing Christmas carols as their teacher guided them from the side. Soon, they were joined by some of the older kids, and I found myself smiling as Penelope came out. She was the only one dressed as a sugarplum fairy, and when she took the center of the stage and started singing solo, my jaw dropped.

My head whipped toward Emily as tears rushed down her face.

"She has an amazing voice," I said in disbelief over how well she could sing for being only nine years old.

"She hasn't sung since Mark died," she cried, wiping the tears away as quickly as she could. I felt the sting prickle my eyes as tears welled up inside.

Twelve
Emily

After the pageant was over, my mom and I took the girls out for ice cream to celebrate their performances and invited Jackson and Sophie to join us. I wasn't sure if it was the right thing to do, only because it felt like we were starting to blur the lines we both had been trying not to cross. Or, more importantly, *I* had been trying not to cross.

The girls laughed and giggled as they ate their sundaes. It was amazing how well the three of them got along, and it made me proud that my girls had taken to Sophie so quickly. She needed this kind of bond and friendship, and I knew that Jackson needed it as well. It was hard to be a single parent, but at least I had my mom to lean on. He didn't have anyone.

After they finished, we packed the girls into my mom's car since she was going to watch them while I attended the company holiday party. They had already planned a sleepover with manicures, pedicures, movies, and junk food, so I didn't have to worry whether they would be bored while I was gone.

"But I want Sophie to come with us," Gracelyn whined as my mom opened the car door for her.

My mom looked at me and raised her brows, silently asking if it was okay. I shrugged and then turned to Jackson, who was talking to Sophie.

"Hey," I said softly, hating to interrupt.

"What's up?" He smiled and held Sophie in front of him with his hands resting on her shoulders. The girls had already changed out of their costumes and were wearing regular clothes.

"The girls are spending the night at my mom's and wanted to see if Sophie could go with them." I hated how nervous I sounded, but it was a big deal. I was asking him to trust us with his niece, and I knew that wasn't an easy thing for him to do. "I know you probably already have a babysitter lined up," I rushed out. "They're welcome to go too if it makes you more comfortable."

He worked his jaw back and forth as he thought about it, then looked down at Sophie.

"What do you think, Squirt? Do you want to go to Megan's house and hang out with Gracelyn and Penelope?"

It sounded weird to hear him call my mom by her name, but it wasn't like he knew her well enough to call her Nana like my girls did.

"Can I?" Sophie beamed up at him, her eyes as wide as saucers.

"If you'd like to, yes."

"I want to! I want to!"

I laughed and nodded to my mom as she helped get Gracelyn buckled in.

"Okay, so what do we do now? Should I follow your mom over and drop her off?"

He looked nervous, which was absolutely adorable on him.

"We can do that," I smiled. "I'll ride with you; that way, you don't get lost if we get separated."

"Sounds good."

I waved at the girls and then waited while he got Sophie secured in the backseat in her booster seat. It was a quick drive to the house, just like everything else in Sugarplum Falls, but I felt like I needed an excuse to spend more time with him.

Once we got there, I led them inside and laughed when Sophie took off to the playroom with the girls without even hesitating.

"Well, I guess I know where I stand," Jackson joked.

"Did you want to call your sitter and let them know to come here?" I asked, feeling my mom's curious gaze on me.

"Yeah, I can do that."

He pulled out his phone and started swiping the screen before my mom interrupted.

"I hope I'm not out of line," she said, "but you don't have to have them come over to watch her here. I'm more than happy to watch Sophie, but I understand if you'd feel more comfortable with someone else being here."

Jackson lowered his phone and smiled.

"I trust you to watch her; I just didn't want to inconvenience you. I had Sunny scheduled to watch her so I can ask her to pick her up and take her to my place if it gets too late. I'm not sure how late the party will go tonight."

"It's not a big deal," my mom answered, holding her hands up to stop him. "She's welcome to stay the night with the girls, or if you'd rather pick her up when you're done, that works too.

And Sunny is more than welcome to come hang out with us too. We just adore her; she does an amazing job with the girls."

"We can always touch base when the girls start winding down," I offered, looking between the two of them.

"That works for me; you know I'm a night owl either way." My mom smiled and patted Jackson's arm. "Now I'm going to go order the pizza before it gets too late. You two better get going, or you're going to miss your own party."

I laughed and looked at Jackson.

"Are you sure you're okay with this?"

He nodded and looked around.

"Yeah, I think so. I mean, if Sophie is comfortable here without me, why should I be worried? She loves hanging out with the girls, and your mom is wonderful with all three of them."

"Well, if you change your mind at any time, you know where she lives," I joked but meant every word.

We said our goodbyes and then left. I asked Jackson to swing by my house real quick so I could change. It was a casual event, but I still wanted to dress up a little bit. Maybe it was because I didn't go out often anymore, or perhaps it was because I secretly felt like this could be a date. Either way, I shook those feelings and rushed to get ready so that we could be the first ones there.

Ten minutes later, I had freshened up my makeup and changed into a pair of skinny jeans and a fitted cream-colored sweater that always flattered my body. I debated whether to wear my winter boots that would keep me warm all night or the sexy stilettos that never got any attention.

When I walked into the living room, I noticed the way Jackson's jaw clenched and his gray eyes darkened when he saw me. Apparently, the heels were the right choice.

By the time we got to the office, a few people were already there and waiting for their drinks at the bar. I was impressed with how smoothly everything had been set up without us having to be there.

I made my way to the office and hung my coat on the rack beside my purse. My body tingled as soon as Jackson approached, our arms brushing against each other as he hung his jacket next to mine.

He looked incredible in the dark-washed denim jeans he was wearing that just so happened to wrap perfectly around his thick thighs and tight ass. But it was the button-down shirt that was casually rolled up to his elbows that had me foaming at the mouth.

I was lost in thought, staring at the ink on his arm that peeked under the fabric, when I heard him clear his throat.

"Everything okay?" he asked, smirking as he lowered his arm and leaned against the wall.

"Yeah, sorry."

He licked his lips as my eyes traveled up to meet his.

"A penny for your thoughts," he offered, tilting his head to the side.

I shook mine, knowing that there was no way I could tell him what I was thinking.

"Fine," he sighed, pushing away from the wall. He took a few steps until he was right in front of me. Gently, he placed his hand on my stomach and pushed my back against the wall, pinning me in place.

He kept his hand on me as he leaned in close and whispered in my ear.

"I'll pay whatever you want if you tell me what you're thinking."

My back arched, and my breathing slowed as I held my breath. I wanted to reach out and touch him. Pull him closer to me and feel his lips on mine. But I couldn't do any of that, no matter how much I wanted it.

"I should walk away and leave you alone," he said quietly, resting his forehead against mine while keeping his hand on my stomach. His fingers grazed lightly, tickling my skin beneath the sweater. "But I can't, Emily. You're like this forbidden fruit, and I want a bite."

I closed my eyes and allowed myself a brief moment to enjoy this.

"I see the way you react to me, Emily. I can tell you feel this too. So, please, tell me what you're thinking. Tell me that I'm not crazy and that I'm not the only one who wants something they can't have."

Before I could overthink it, I reached up and wrapped my arms around his neck, pulling him closer to me. I parted my lips, eager to taste his as they trailed lightly over mine. I wanted more, but he was teasing me, gently running his tongue over my lips and then nipping them.

I moaned and let my head fall back as he took control. He gripped the back of my neck and held me in place as his mouth crashed down over mine, kissing me with more passion than I'd ever felt before. My legs trembled as I fought the urge to wrap them around his waist. He brought out a side in me that I didn't know was there until now.

We were full-blown making out, hands grabbing at each other's bodies, desperate for more, when he suddenly pulled away.

His eyes were wild as he looked at me and scrubbed a hand down his face.

My chest was heaving as I tried to catch my breath and calm myself down. I felt alive and wanted more than what he'd given me.

"Fuck," he muttered and covered his mouth with his hand. His lips were as swollen as mine, and I wanted to feel them on my body again.

"I'm sorry," I blurted out, even though I wasn't sorry at all. As much as I thought I would regret it, I didn't. Though I knew that part would probably come later after the high of kissing Jackson wore off. "I didn't mean to...." I let my words trail off, unsure of what I was apologizing for.

He narrowed his eyes and tilted his head.

Suddenly his features softened, and he reached out and brushed a thumb over my cheek.

"Emily, I'm not upset that it happened. Trust me, I would stay in here all night and do that if I could."

I giggled and covered my mouth.

"I'm frustrated because I'm the owner of the company, and I need to get down there to greet everyone as they get here, and I can't do that with this fucking erection."

He looked down at his jeans, and I gasped when I saw the thick outline of what he was talking about.

He was right; that was a problem. A *big* problem.

Thirteen
Jackson

It was painfully uncomfortable walking around, greeting employees while trying to block out the memories of Emily's lips on mine a few minutes ago. Thankfully, my erection had subsided, so I didn't have to worry about the attention I was sure to draw with the snake in my pants.

We'd freshened up—Emily more than me since I'd smeared the red lipstick she was wearing—and made our way down to where the party was. I could hardly believe how easily everything had come together. The bar was set up at the reception desk, with a line of people waiting to get a drink. Across from that were the food tables where the buffet was already set up. Since we didn't have a large kitchen—or a stove—it was easier to do the food as a buffet instead of plated dinner. It also saved Carmen from having to bring wait staff to serve the dishes.

Once everyone had their drinks and was situated in the conference room, I took my seat at the front and motioned for Emily to join me. I was worried that she wouldn't know anyone besides Bea and me, but I saw her laughing and talking with a few of the ladies from accounting. Then I remembered that Sugarplum Falls was a small town, and she'd probably met almost everyone at some point in the time she'd been here.

I gave a brief speech, thanking everyone for being such an important part of our team and raised my glass. After that, I allowed Carmen to take the lead in getting everyone through the buffet line to get their food. Emily and I waited until everyone else went through and then fixed our plates.

"Everything looks delicious," I commented, picking up a piece of roasted chicken.

Even though the food was served buffet-style, it was exactly what I'd expect from a five-star restaurant. Emily wasn't lying when she said that Carmen was a very talented chef.

"I can't wait to dive in." She smiled and added a baked potato to her plate with roasted garlic cloves and thick-cut sirloin.

I added a serving of green beans and grabbed a roll before accepting that my plate was too full to add more food.

We set our food down on the table, and then I pulled Emily's chair out for her. Her smile beamed at me, and suddenly, I wondered if everyone would think something was happening between us. I wasn't treating her like an employee; I was treating her like a date.

I cleared my throat and sat down, trying to remind myself to act like the CEO and not some horny frat boy.

Emily grabbed the linen napkin beside her plate and unfolded it before setting it on her lap. Unfortunately, the room was more crowded than I had imagined, and we were sitting close enough to each other that I felt her fingers brush against my thigh.

I pulled away sharply, noticing the way she flinched in response. I wasn't trying to be a dick, but I was seriously struggling to figure out where the line was that I wasn't supposed to be crossing. It was like being drunk and trying to pass a sobriety test.

We ate as those around us talked and carried on the conversation. I tried my best to participate, but my head was a foggy mess with thoughts of Emily occupying every corner of it. Carmen made her way through, checking in to see how everyone was doing. I loved that she didn't just hide in the kitchen and consider her job done but that she was actually engaging with people and making sure there was plenty for everyone.

Once dinner was over, we'd moved the tables and chairs from the conference room to the waiting area where the buffet set up had been taken down, and the tables now featured an assortment of delectable desserts. Emily had suggested creating a relaxing environment in the waiting area for those who wanted to sit and visit without having to yell over the sound of music. We'd hired a DJ who was currently setting up and converting the space into a dance floor.

When I walked up to the bar, Emily was mingling with a few employees in the waiting area.

"What can I get for you, sir?"

I checked out the collection of bottles on the shelf behind her, debating on what to get.

"I'll have a whiskey sour, please."

She nodded and turned to make the drink. I was looking down at my phone, debating reaching out to Megan to check on Sophie, when someone came up and stood next to me.

"Care to dance?" Emily asked, looking up at me with sparkling green eyes.

I shoved my phone back into my pocket and grabbed the drink that was handed to me.

"Do you want a drink?" I offered, nodding to the bartender who was standing there watching us.

"Umm. I'll have a glass of Moscato, please."

The bartender smiled and poured Emily's drink. Once she had it in hand, I placed mine on her lower back and guided her away so the others who had joined us could order their drinks.

I wanted nothing more than to take Emily back to my office and finish what we'd started earlier, but that wasn't an option. So, against my better judgment, I let her lead me to the dance floor that had been set up.

She set our drinks on one of the corner tables, grabbed my hands, and pulled me out into the middle, where everyone else was dancing. Thankfully, it was an upbeat song that didn't require any close touching. As far as anyone was concerned, I was just dancing with a handful of employees. Nothing wrong with that. I was just being a good boss and interacting with my coworkers.

A few songs passed, and I thought I was in the clear until suddenly the DJ changed it to a slow song. Emily smiled and extended her hand to me. I didn't want to embarrass her, so I took it and pulled her into me as we moved in a slow rhythm.

It was as if everyone else had disappeared, and it was just me and Emily on the dance floor. I closed my eyes and allowed myself to breathe in her scent. Her fingers gripped my shoulders tighter as I tried to keep my hands on her waist and not her ass, which was where I really wanted to put them.

She shifted, and I felt her breasts press against my chest. It was hard to keep myself from being unaffected by her when everything running through me right now screamed for me to take her up to my office and fuck her.

I could feel my dick start to harden, so I pushed her away and stepped back.

"I'm sorry," I rushed out, running a hand through my hair. "I have to go. I'll call you an Uber when you're ready. Just text me and let me know."

"Okay," she stammered. "I can go with you—"

"No," I interrupted, startling her. "Please let your mom know I'm heading over to pick Sophie up."

I didn't wait for her to say anything else before I turned and walked out, ignoring the whispers and curious looks around me.

Fourteen
Emily

After Jackson's vanishing act on Saturday, I hadn't spoken to him since. I'd texted my mom to let her know he was on his way to pick up Sophie but didn't answer her other questions when I got home an hour later. I knew it would only encourage more gossip if I rushed out after him, so I stuck it out and tried to mingle with the few people I knew.

When that failed, I found Carmen in the breakroom and decided to help her pack up her stuff. Instead of texting Jackson about a ride, I grabbed one with Carmen and left after the other employees cleared out. It wasn't a late night, which turned out to be a good thing, given how tired I was.

Sunday was supposed to be a relaxing day with the girls, but we ended up shopping most of the day for gifts for their friends and my mom. It was two weeks until Christmas, and I was still scrambling to get stuff done, though I was thankful we'd gotten the tree up and the house decorated. We got home that evening and shoved the bags under the tree so I could wrap them later, and then ordered a pizza and called it a night.

By Monday morning, I felt awkward about how things had been left between Jackson and me. It felt like I had whiplash from his constant back-and-forth of mixed signals. First, he pinned me against the wall and kissed me, and then flinched when I accidentally brushed his leg under the table at dinner. After that, I got him to dance with me, and it seemed like he was having a good time until a slow song came on, and he seemed to freak out again.

I expected—or rather hoped—that he would text me at some point so we could talk about what happened, but there was nothing but silence. I considered texting him but didn't want to be the one to make the first move. It was childish, but I refused to do anything until I knew what was going on inside his head.

When I got to the office, I was surprised that I beat him there. Granted, I had only worked for Mason, Inc. for three days, but so far, Jackson had always been there when I got in.

I went about the morning the same way I had last week. I started a fresh pot of coffee and turned on the laptop Jackson had given me while it brewed. A handful of emails popped up in my inbox, which surprised me, given that I hadn't been there long enough for people to send me anything.

A quick glance showed that the majority of them were from employees, thanking Jackson and me for throwing such a wonderful holiday party. I smiled and felt a sense of pride wash over me from a job well done.

I got up and headed to the breakroom, desperate for another cup of coffee. I'd already had one at home while getting the girls ready for school. They only had a few days left, and then they'd be out for Christmas break. I was a bit jealous that I wouldn't get to spend time with them, but I was thankful that my mom would be there.

The coffee trickled slowly into the pot while I tapped my foot impatiently.

"You sure you need more caffeine?" Jackson asked, startling me as he stood beside me. "You look like you're going to take off at any moment."

I wanted to respond to him, but suddenly I didn't know what to say. I was an equal combination of angry with him for practically ghosting me and hurt that he'd led me on only to change his mind about it. Either way, neither of those moods made me want to talk to him.

Instead, I huffed out a frustrated breath and grabbed the handle as soon as the last few drops of coffee landed in the pot.

With as steady of a hand as I could muster, I poured the mug full and then set the pot back on the warmer.

I didn't bother to ask if he wanted a cup. Sure I was technically his assistant, but as far as I was concerned, he could fix his own damn coffee today.

I went back to the office, not bothering to look behind me as I heard his footsteps follow. I set the cup down on the coaster and then pulled myself up to the table, focusing on the emails that were awaiting a reply.

Jackson came in a few seconds later, his gaze sending heat waves through my body. He sat down at his desk but didn't try to initiate another conversation with me. Instead, he turned his attention to his computer, but I still felt his eyes wander over to me more often than they should.

By eleven, I had responded to the emails that came through and started a list of options for the booth Mason, Inc. had signed up to host for the Frosty Fest. I reached out to Jasmin and confirmed which items were still left and which ones had already been taken.

I heard movement as Jackson walked around the office and then headed down the hallway. I sighed a breath of relief that he was gone for a moment, and I could finally think.

I'd tried hard to focus all morning, but it was damn near impossible every time I heard him speak on the phone or shift in his chair. I wanted to talk to him, but I couldn't bring myself to push my wounded ego aside to do so.

Fifteen minutes later, he returned to the office with to-go bags. He closed the office door and then headed straight for the conference table.

I looked up and then immediately cleared my stuff out of the way to make room for him.

"Sorry, I can get out of here so you can eat."

I stood up to leave, but Jackson moved and blocked me in.

"I ordered lunch for both of us. I'd like to talk to you and thought maybe we could do so while we ate."

I pulled nervously at the bottom of my shirt, looking down at the table, so I didn't have to look at him.

"Please, Emily."

He lifted my chin with his finger, his eyes locking on mine as soon as I looked up.

I swallowed hard, trying to force away the feelings that were lingering at the surface.

"Have lunch with me. I need to apologize for how I acted on Saturday, and I can't stand the thought of you not talking to me."

My stomach growled, betraying me.

"Okay," I whispered, pulling away from his touch, though I didn't want to.

We sat down, and Jackson unpacked our food, setting a burger and fries in front of me. I smiled when I realized he remembered my order from the other day and got me my favorite comfort food.

"You didn't have to do this," I said, looking across the table at him.

"Yes, I did. I feel like a complete ass after what happened the other night. And trust me, buying you lunch doesn't even begin to express how sorry I am."

I picked up the cheeseburger and took a bite, allowing him time to continue talking since I had no idea what to say.

He raked a hand through his hair and looked at me.

"You drive me crazy," he blurted out, startling me so much that I choked on the bite that I was eating.

I covered my mouth and coughed as I tried to force the food down.

"Excuse me?" I asked, tilting my head at him.

"You heard me," he chuckled and pushed a fry into his mouth. His plump lips looked sinfully good as he chewed, so I forced myself to look away.

"You drive me absolutely crazy, and I find myself stuck in hell because I don't know what to do. I've tried everything I can to avoid crossing that line, Emily. I want you in ways that I shouldn't. I want to do things to your body that makes me hard just thinking about them. I want to say fuck it, that it doesn't matter that I'm your boss and you're my employee, but I can't. There are so many lines that I shouldn't cross, and suddenly, they're blurry. I don't know what to do," he sighed heavily.

I pulled in a deep breath and held it for a few seconds while I tried to compose my thoughts.

I'd spent a lot of time this weekend thinking about what happened between us. Part of me loved feeling wanted and the high that I felt when he touched me. I'd felt alive and wanted more—much more than what he'd given me.

But then the guilt would wash over me again, and I hated myself for cheating on Mark, though I knew it wasn't really cheating. I couldn't shake the feeling that I'd done something wrong, and that was a hard thing to process.

Mark and I talked about what the future would look like for me if he didn't get better. It wasn't a conversation I wanted to have, and I tried to shut it down every time he started. But after his last round of chemo, he'd forced me to have it.

I remembered sitting next to him on the couch, curling into his side as much as possible without hurting him. He was so frail that I was scared to touch him at that point. But he held me and told me how he wanted to make sure that I always knew how much he loved me and that he wanted me to find love again. He promised me that I was destined for a life of happiness and that he wanted me to promise that I would make an effort to date again and find someone to spend the rest of my life with.

While I technically had Mark's blessing to move on, it felt like it was too soon. Even though I knew he wasn't coming back, I couldn't push myself to accept that he was really gone.

I cleared my throat and lowered my shoulders.

"If it's any consolation, you drive me crazy, too," I admitted, earning a cheeky grin from him.

"Is that so?"

"Yes," I laughed. "Your mood swings have given me whiplash," I joked, rubbing my neck dramatically.

"I'll add a 90-minute massage to your holiday bonus for all of the trouble." He winked, and I felt the warmth return between my thighs.

"Holiday bonus?"

"Yeah, all employees get a thousand-dollar bonus at Christmas. It usually gets paid out two weeks before, but I was a little distracted and forgot to have Bea put it in last week. If you have direct deposit, it should be in your account as of this morning."

"A thousand dollars?" My jaw dropped.

He nodded slowly and watched my reaction.

"But I've only been here like three days," I said, shaking my head to clear the fog.

"Doesn't matter. You're still an employee." He took a bite of his burger and then wiped his mouth with his napkin. "Plus, you did a killer job with the holiday party. You more than earned it."

I blinked several times, trying to wrap my head around the news.

"Wow. Thank you so much. You have no idea how much that means to me."

He smiled and kept eating while I finally picked up my burger and took a bite.

"Does that mean you're not mad at me anymore?" he asked with a playful tone.

I bit into a French fry and waited before answering.

"I guess you're off the hook this time. But I am going to ask if I can leave a few minutes early today. I want to get over to Waldon's before they close so I can grab a few more things from the girls' wish lists."

I had tried to remember everything that was on them after spending the entire weekend trying to find them. And it wasn't like I could ask the girls what was on them since I'd said that I sent them to the North Pole. The lists weren't for me; they were for Santa.

A faint blush crept up Jackson's cheeks as he winced.

"Okay, try not to be mad at me again," he said cautiously.

I narrowed my eyes and set my burger down.

"Why? What did you do?"

"I had good intentions, I swear." He got up and walked over to the coat closet.

I watched as he opened it and pulled out four large bags from Waldon's. He brought them over and set them down in front of me.

"What's all that?"

He swallowed hard, his Adam's apple bobbing up and down.

"I, um, I kinda went back in and purchased the stuff that you put back last week."

"What?" I gasped, placing a hand over my heart. "Why did you do that?"

I wondered if maybe he had bought it for Sophie, assuming she would like some of the same stuff as the girls.

"Honestly? I couldn't stand the thought of you having to pick and choose what gifts to buy your girls. I know I shouldn't have done that without asking, but I wanted them to have everything on their list. I was going to drop it off on Christmas Eve and try to sneak off before anyone saw me, but since you're planning to go buy stuff, I figured I better tell you now."

My heart hammered in my chest as my throat tightened with emotion.

"Jackson," I whispered, blinking away the tears. "You didn't have to do that."

"I know. I wanted to."

Before I could stop it, a tear slid down my cheek. He reached over and gently brushed it away with his thumb.

"I know I've been overstepping a lot lately, and I'm sorry. If you want me to take it back to the store, I can. I just didn't want to risk them not having it."

I wiped the rest of the tears with the backs of my hands and stood up to face him.

"You have the biggest heart of anyone I've ever met, Jackson." I reached up and cupped the sides of his face, debating whether to kiss him or not.

I knew that he was already struggling with whatever this thing was between us, but he wasn't the only one.

"I can still play Santa and drop them off on Christmas Eve if you want," he murmured, bringing his mouth closer to mine.

"Does that mean I get to sit on your lap and tell you what I want?" I teased, brushing my lips against his.

"If you sit on my lap, I can *guarantee* you'll get what you want." A low growl escaped his lips before they locked onto mine.

Fifteen
Jackson

By the time the weekend rolled around, I was up to my eyeballs in planning for the Sugarplum Falls Frosty Fest. Emily had taken the lead on it and coordinated with her friend Jasmin to see what they needed since we were the last vendor to submit our plans for the event.

It turned out that the locals were on top of grabbing the fun things first, and those who were crafty signed up for what looked like the easy stuff. By the time we got situated, Jasmin had confirmed that the only thing they needed was someone to be Santa and Mrs. Claus. Apparently, the couple who usually did had come down with the flu and left them shorthanded, which left an opening for us to fill.

Sunny was going to help take Sophie to see Santa while I was working the event on Saturday, and I hoped it would be an easy way to find out what she wanted for Christmas. I'd asked her for her list, but she looked at me like I was crazy and then ran off to watch some cartoon with a blue dog that wouldn't stop singing.

I asked Emily about it, and she said not to worry; some kids weren't big into making lists for Santa. It could be that it wasn't something she and my sister did, or she was just too young to put a list together herself. Emily promised to have Penelope hint around until she got some ideas about what

Sophie was into, but I figured having Sophie visit Santa was a surefire way to get a direct answer.

I was nervous that she would recognize me, but Jasmin said that as long as I didn't say much other than, *what would you like this year for Christmas*, that I would be fine. Most of the kids would be too excited, and if I got nervous, Mrs. Claus could ask for me.

Emily helped me get dressed before she rushed off to put on her costume. When she came out of the bathroom, I stopped what I was doing and smiled.

She looked adorable in the red velvet dress that was padded to the extreme to make her look plump and round. Her cheeks had plenty of blush to make them rosy, but I hated how the small glasses hid her beautiful green eyes.

"You look great," I commented, still unable to take my eyes off her.

"Thanks," she laughed and smoothed her hands over her stomach. "I feel so silly in it. But thankfully, my hair is short enough to hide it easily under this wig."

"I would say it's only a few hours, but it's the whole day," I laughed. "But at least you don't have to wear fake eyebrows and a beard."

"True, but you make a handsome-looking Santa."

"Is that so?" I lowered my voice and felt the flutters in my stomach.

"Mmm hmm."

"Have you been a good girl this year?" I stepped closer to her, enjoying the flirty banter between us when the door opened, and Jasmin walked in.

"Alright, you two, you ready?"

"As ready as I'll ever be," Emily said, taking a deep breath and blowing it out.

"Look at you two! This is perfect!" Jasmin exclaimed, leading her out by the elbow as I followed after them.

We waved at the crowd as we walked down the narrow walkway to the stage they had set up for Santa. It was lined with Christmas trees lit up by brightly colored lights and beautifully wrapped presents underneath. An oversized chair sat in the middle for Santa, with a stool beside it for Mrs. Claus. I was thankful that Emily was right there with me, but I also wished we didn't have to do this. There were a million other things that I would rather do today instead—like finish my Christmas shopping and get presents wrapped while Sophie wasn't around. Christmas was officially a week away, and I had so much left to do. Thankfully, I'd been able to get a tree and some lights up, so I wasn't totally slacking.

Once Emily and I were situated, the elves rushed around the stage before they started bringing the kids on stage to have their picture taken with Santa. It was going to be a long day, but at least we would get a thirty-minute break for lunch, and I could have some time alone with her.

The first few kids were older, which seemed to help the younger ones in line, who seemed a little nervous about meeting Santa. We only had a few who cried and screamed bloody murder when I held them, but then Emily started talking to them, and they soon calmed down. She was like some sort of child whisperer, and I found myself wanting to have a million of them with her.

"Alright, guys, that's it for now. Santa and Mrs. Claus are going to get some lunch, and we encourage you to do the same. There are plenty of food options, including some food trucks on the north side, as well as the main food court. We'll be back at one o'clock and ready to meet those sweet faces we haven't seen yet." Jasmin waved at the crowd as they dispersed before coming to talk to us.

"Since you guys have a short break, we took the liberty of having food brought over for you. There's a handful of options in the break room if you want to help yourselves. We'll see you at one." She smiled and rushed off, leaving Emily and me to ourselves.

I followed Emily to the breakroom, thankful that this event was held inside the mall and that we didn't have to brave the blistery cold winter storm that was raging outside. It was going to be hell when we left, but for now, we were warm and cozy inside.

There was no one else in the breakroom but a large assortment of food waiting for us. I knew that the other staff would be back soon to eat as well, but for now, it was just us.

I grabbed a plate and handed one to Emily before walking along the table and deciding what I wanted to eat.

I mean, I knew what I wanted to eat, but that wasn't an option right now.

Things between Emily and me had been great this week, and the flirting was constant. Even though we both agreed that we shouldn't act on our attraction right now, that didn't stop it from constantly simmering on the surface.

Emily filled her plate with a few things and then sat down at one of the tables in the corner, where I joined her once I had my food. We ate in silence for a few minutes until a handful of elves came in and joined us.

They were chattering about something that happened at school, and it dawned on me that they were probably middle school or high school kids who were volunteering or got roped into helping by their parents. I knew they weren't real elves, but I was quite impressed with how short they were for adults until I learned the truth.

"Have you heard from Sunny yet?" Emily asked as she opened a bag of potato chips and popped one in her mouth.

"Yeah, they just got here twenty minutes ago. She's going to make sure she gets Sophie in line when it opens again."

"Are you nervous?"

"Nervous?" I tilted my head and took a bite of the turkey and provolone sandwich.

"That she might recognize you." Her eyes lit up as she smiled. *God, she was beautiful.*

"A little," I admitted. "The last thing I want to do is ruin something for her if she figures out that it's me."

I looked up cautiously, wording my sentence since I didn't know how old the elves were or if they still believed in Santa.

"Don't worry; a lot of the kids around town understand that he has helpers this time of year."

I smiled and felt more relaxed about it. I still hated that I didn't know much about what traditions, if any, Sophie and my sister had. Whenever I brought up Cammy, Sophie would get sad and shut down. I'd been taking her to a therapist Emily recommended, but we hadn't had much luck getting her to talk about her mom or what had happened.

We finished our lunches with just a few minutes to spare for a bathroom break before making our way back to the stage.

I looked around, trying to spot Sunny and Sophie in the crowd, but I couldn't find them. I really hoped that they would get there soon because the line was already long, and the Santa part of the festival was supposed to be over at four.

Emily was talking to Jasmin while I sat down in the giant throne and tried to get comfortable. The elves came rushing back out, giggling about something until I saw one of them pointing to a piece of mistletoe that was suddenly hanging right over Emily and me. I arched an eyebrow, wondering if it would move the fake one as well.

One of the shorter elves covered her mouth and looked away, confirming it had worked.

Rascals.

Jasmin walked to the middle of the stage while Emily sat down on the stool next to me and smoothed her dress. It was weird to be this turned on by someone that currently looked like an eighty-year-old grandma, but apparently, I had some sort of Mrs. Claus kink I never knew about.

Before she could start talking, someone in the crowd began chanting, '*kiss, kiss, kiss*.' Jasmin turned toward us, caught sight of the mistletoe, and shrugged. More people joined in on the chant until it became loud enough for everyone in the mall to hear.

I looked over at Emily, trying to see how she felt about it.

She completely played up the part of Mrs. Claus, acting bashful as she tried to hide her face behind her hand. With a glove shielding her face from the crowd, she smiled and subtly nodded to let me know we should do it.

Pretending to be upset about it, I playfully shook a finger at the elves and then got up and stood next to Emily.

The crowd cheered louder, continuing their chant about us kissing.

I leaned in and snaked a hand behind Emily's waist, gently pulling her in for a G-rated kiss.

She pressed her lips firmly against mine, and I could tell she was struggling to keep this tame, just like I was.

"The offer still stands for you to sit on my cock and tell me what you want me to give you for Christmas," I growled quietly in her ear as I pulled away.

She gasped and swatted at my arm, earning some additional cheers from the adults in the crowd, who clearly understood what was happening on stage.

I sat down on the throne, feeling mighty proud of myself for getting Emily so worked up. But then I looked into the crowd and spotted Megan in line with Gracelyn and Penelope. Gracelyn was talking to her grandma and hadn't seen the kiss on stage; however, Penelope saw everything. Given that she no longer believed in Santa, I knew that Emily had told her she would be playing Mrs. Claus today and wouldn't be able to go shopping with them.

Even from far away, I saw the tears in her eyes before she stormed off and didn't bother to look back.

Sixteen
Emily

"Need to talk," Jackson gritted through his teeth loud enough for me to hear. His face was oddly tight as he tried to force a smile while hiding what he was saying to me.

"What's wrong?" I asked behind a fake smile, waving at the kids in line.

"Penelope."

"What?" I tried not to look at him but felt my brow furrow as I turned toward him.

He briefly met my eyes before smiling at the little boy heading across the stage to us.

"Kiss. Mad. Left."

The smile on my face felt harder to keep as my stomach dropped.

No.

I hadn't bothered to talk to the girls about the possibility of me dating again after their dad died, and honestly, it was because I never saw a reason for it. Why bring them additional things to worry about or be upset over when I didn't even have any prospects in town?

But things changed so suddenly with Jackson that I hadn't had a chance to figure it out myself, let alone try to explain it to them.

I knew how temperamental Penelope was these days, and her therapist had confirmed that she'd also noticed some changes in her. She was angrier than usual, and while we understood that anger was a part of grieving, I wasn't content chalking it up to just that.

The little boy climbed up on Jackson's lap and rattled off a list of things he wanted, but I found myself unable to focus. My eyes quickly scanned the crowd, looking for Penelope. How long had it been since she left? Did my mom go after her?

I desperately wanted to climb off the stage and go find my daughter, but I knew that I couldn't. There was too much on the line to risk doing that.

For one, it would embarrass Penelope, and two, it would out Mrs. Claus to Gracelyn, as well as the other kids.

So, I forced a fake smile and tried to act calm, even though I felt like I was going to jump out of my skin.

I was so busy obsessing over where she was that I hadn't heard Jackson clear his throat the first time. He did it again, this time louder, getting my attention.

"Three o'clock."

I followed his gaze until I spotted my mom with Penelope off to the side of where everyone was in line to see Santa.

Relieved, I let out a sigh and relaxed for a moment until I realized that Gracelyn wasn't with them. Just as I started to panic again, I heard Jackson cough and turned my head. He nodded to the line where Sunny was waiting with Sophie and Gracelyn.

It was an overly emotional and exhausting few minutes, and suddenly, I couldn't wait until this was over. I wanted to go see my girls and make sure that they were doing okay.

Jackson passed quickly through the next few kids until Sophie was next in line. I could feel the tension radiating off him from where I sat on the stool. I wanted to comfort and remind him that he didn't need to say much, but I was too late.

"Hey, little girl, what would you like for Christmas this year?" he asked a little too loudly and sounding like himself.

Sophie pulled her brows down in confusion, stopping just short of the throne.

As if realizing what he'd done, he turned his head and started coughing.

Seeing an opportunity, I hopped off the stool and kneeled in front of her.

"Hey, sweetie. Santa has a tickle in his throat, which makes it hard for him to talk right now. Do you want to have a seat on his lap so that nice elf over there can take your picture?"

She nodded and wrapped her arms protectively around her waist. Sunny stood off to the side, talking to one of the elves.

I helped Sophie up onto Jackson's lap and then smiled as we posed for the picture. Once they gave us the thumbs up that they got it, I turned to Sophie and kneeled to her level again.

"Since Santa needs to save his voice, do you want to tell me what you want for Christmas?"

She looked up at him, then back at me, and shook her head. I glanced at him, unsure of what to do. Obviously, we didn't want to bully the kid into telling us, but I also knew how important it was to Jackson to find out.

"Did you make a list for Santa that you wanted to share instead?" I offered, wondering if maybe Sunny had been helping her with one.

She shook her head again, and I noticed the tears well in her eyes.

"Honey," I said softly, my heart breaking for her. "It's okay."

She curled her head into Jackson's beard and cried harder. He closed his eyes and wrapped his arms around her, holding her as if there weren't a hundred other kids in line, waiting for their turns.

A few minutes passed by before she pulled away and wiped her eyes.

"Are you okay, sweetie?" I asked softly, holding my hand up to stop the elf that was heading our way to tell us we needed to move on to the next kid and keep the line moving.

"No, I'm sad."

"Why? What's wrong?"

It was a stupid question to ask, given that I knew the heartache she was suffering. But I asked anyway.

When she didn't answer me, I pushed harder.

"Is there something you want for Christmas that you're afraid to ask for?"

She nodded.

Oh, finally, we were getting somewhere.

"What do you want? Santa can make *a lot* of things happen. Almost like magic." My eyes widened as I said it.

As much as I could predict after being a mother for so long, I couldn't have imagined what she was about to say.

"I want my mommy back."

Seventeen
Jackson

By the time four o'clock rolled around, and we saw the last kid, I was mentally and physically exhausted. I couldn't wait to get out of the stuffy Santa suit, but more importantly, I couldn't wait to find Sunny and Sophie.

Her wish to Santa shattered my heart. While I had plenty of money and was used to being able to buy whatever I wanted, I'd finally reached a point where no amount of money could buy what she wanted.

I had noticed the tears in Emily's eyes and knew she was as upset about Sophie's wish as I was. While I'd been worried that she was going to request something super hard to get, I wasn't prepared for her to ask for something that no one could give her.

We gave a final wave to the crowd as Jasmin escorted us back to the changing area. She thanked us profusely for stepping in and helping, then ran off to assist a vendor.

The festival was scheduled to go on until ten o'clock, which gave us plenty of time to walk around and enjoy it. I hoped that Sophie would still want to enjoy the festival, but I wasn't counting on it.

Emily grabbed her pile of clothes and went to the bathroom to change while I stripped out of my Santa suit in the main breakroom. No one else was in there, and it wasn't like I was getting naked. Granted, the clothes I had on were gross and probably smelled like sweat, but that's why I had a clean pair to change into once Emily was out of the bathroom.

A few minutes later, Emily came out wearing a pair of fitted jeans, and a navy-blue turtleneck pulled tightly across her chest. She wore ankle boots that didn't have a heel like the ones she wore last weekend to the party, but they were sexy, nonetheless.

She smiled and walked past me to hang the Mrs. Claus outfit on the garment rack in the corner.

"You look nice," I commented as I slipped past her to the bathroom.

I cleaned up the best I could and applied a fresh layer of deodorant, just to be on the safe side. When I'd picked what to wear today, I might have been looking to impress Emily and decided on dark-washed denim jeans and a white button-down shirt. I'd noticed her checking me out a handful of times over the past week or so, but she seemed to really enjoy what I'd worn to the holiday party, so I aimed for that style again.

Once I was done, I walked out and noticed that Emily was sitting on the arm of the couch, chewing her nail nervously as she looked at her phone. She looked up, and I saw something in her eyes that punched me in the gut.

"What's wrong?" I asked, holding the dirty clothes that I'd folded and planned to run out to the car.

"My mom said that Penelope is still upset over that kiss."

"I'm so sorry, Emily. I didn't even think about what would happen if she saw us."

"I know," she breathed heavily, then planted her hands on her thighs and stood up. "I just need to sit down and talk with her."

I nodded and struggled with what to say to that.

"Do you want me to be there when you do? Maybe I can help explain that it was just part of the job." I shrugged.

"But was it?" She tilted her head and questioned me.

She was right, and I knew it.

"Look, Jackson," she sighed. "I like you, and I know that you like me. We're both aware of the chemistry between us and know how attracted to each other we are. But I can't do anything if it upsets my girls. I'm sorry, but they've been through enough already, and I can't put them through more heartache or stress. It's just not fair."

I swallowed hard and looked down at my boots.

"So what are you saying?"

"I think we need to stop whatever this is between us for now. At least until I can talk to the girls and see how they feel about it."

"And if they don't approve?"

Her face reddened as she tucked a strand of hair behind her ear.

I pulled my lips together and nodded.

"Got it."

Her head whipped up as she looked at me with tears in her eyes.

"Jackson, please," she whispered as I turned and walked out the door.

Eighteen
Emily

The Frosty Fest was fun, but I couldn't help but feel like something was missing. Granted, it was the first year that I'd attended one, but I had spent the past week imagining Jackson and Sophie being here with us.

It was odd how quickly they seemed to fuse together with my family, but it just felt natural when we were all together. My girls adored Sophie, and she seemed to love them just as much as they loved her. I'd never seen three girls laugh and giggle as much as they did when they were together.

But seeing how upset Penelope was over my kiss with Jackson, I couldn't just ignore it. I knew that it would be hard for them the first time I decided to start dating again, but I honestly didn't expect it to happen so soon. Nor did I expect it to happen with someone who I'd just met, let alone around Christmas time.

My mom took Gracelyn to go shopping for Penelope and me, a tradition I used to do with Mark, while I took Penelope to shop for them. While I knew that we were supposed to be finding the last few gifts for each other, I understood that my mom was giving me an opportunity to have a one-on-one conversation with Penelope about what had happened.

I grabbed us some hot chocolate and a mint-fudge brownie from one of the kiosks and led her over to one of the tables in the corner, where it was quieter.

We sat down, and I hated how on edge I felt. I knew that it wasn't just my own nerves about having this conversation with her but that I was feeling the attitude coming from her without her saying anything. Ugh, could the teenage years really be worse than this?

"So, I want to talk to you about something," I said slowly, wrapping my hands around the to-go cup to help quell the chill pushing through me.

She stared at me with a blank expression and made no effort to reach for her cup or the treats sitting between us.

"Okay," I sighed, forcing my shoulders down so I appeared more relaxed than I was. "I know you were upset earlier when you saw Jackson and me kiss."

Her eyes whipped up to mine before anger flashed through them, and she looked away.

I reached a hand across the table and squeezed hers.

"It's okay to talk to me, Nel. Just like it's okay to be upset."

She looked everywhere but at me, not bothering to reciprocate the physical interaction.

Okay, deep breaths. You can handle this. She's just a kid. You literally brought her into this world, don't let her intimidate you.

"This would be a lot easier if you would talk to me," I blurted out, immediately feeling remorseful of the tone I'd used.

"Easier for who?" she asked angrily.

I pulled my hand back and set the to-go cup to the side so I didn't accidentally fling it off the table.

My eyebrows rose in response, but I forced myself to keep my cool. If I wanted her to talk to me, I needed to be a little more lenient.

"First—watch your tone. I know you're angry, but you don't talk to me that way. Second, I want you to talk to me and tell me what's going on. I know that it's more than just the kiss you saw earlier. Please talk to me, Nel."

She rolled her eyes and looked away.

"There's nothing to talk about."

I inhaled deeply and slowly blew it out.

"Then why are you so angry?"

Her jaw clenched, and her fingers turned white as she laced them together.

"It's okay to be angry," I continued, lifting my cup to my mouth to take a drink.

"Says who?"

I shrugged.

"Everyone."

She finally looked at me.

"Everyone gets angry at some point, Nel. It's natural, and we couldn't stop it if we tried. But it's what we do with that anger that matters."

Her face softened slightly, and she finally reached for the to-go cup of hot chocolate that was waiting for her.

"What do you mean?"

"I mean that all of us get angry for different reasons, but how we handle it is what's important. You can either learn from whatever angered you and then move on, or you can let it be the only thing you focus on and allow it to consume you. Either way, you're going to feel it. But you're the only one who can decide how you move past it."

She slowly sipped the beverage, her hazel eyes reminding me so much of her dad.

"Are you angry?" she asked quietly.

I pulled my head back slightly, caught off guard by her question.

"Umm," I breathed slowly. "I don't know that I'm mad about anything right now. But I get angry plenty of times."

"Do you stay angry?"

I wasn't sure how to answer this for her. Was I supposed to be honest and admit that I was still angry about losing Mark? Or did I try to set a good example for her and lie about it?

"I don't know," I offered. "I mean, I guess I'm still angry about some things, but I try not to let them rule my life or impact my days."

She nodded and started looking around again.

"Is that why you kissed Jackson? Because you're not angry over daddy dying anymore?"

I leaned back in my chair and felt my heart sink.

Nineteen
Jackson

Sunday was spent at home, in our pajamas, as we watched Christmas movies. I was thankful that Sunny had suggested that I sign up for some streaming services, so I had more stuff for Sophie to watch. In all fairness, she didn't watch a ton of TV, but I liked that there were at least some kid-friendly options for her to choose from now.

She giggled as the Grinch and Max tiptoed around, plotting out their plan to steal Christmas while I tried to figure out what to get her. Christmas was officially less than a week away, and I'd never felt more stressed in my life.

It wasn't just the worry of finding the perfect gifts for Sophie that was bothering me; it was how things had ended between Emily and me yesterday. I knew that she wanted to protect her girls and save them from possible heartache, but at the same time, it felt like she was willing to overlook her own happiness to do so.

Falling in love was a gamble when kids were involved, and I could now see that. I wouldn't want Sophie to get attached to someone just to have them walk out of her life so I could get where she was coming from. Either way, it was frustrating, and there didn't seem to be a right answer because it was more than just me and Emily involved.

While she continued watching the movie, curled up on the couch with her favorite blanket, I grabbed my laptop and worked on some of the contracts that I needed to submit this week. Thankfully, I was close to being caught up, and then I could enjoy the holidays. But that didn't mean my mind was worry free like it usually would be after getting work stuff out of the way. I was now facing a million different things to worry about, and that felt all-consuming.

By six, I'd ordered a pizza and sat down with Sophie at the table to eat. She wasn't a picky eater, but I also didn't imagine she would willingly eat a pizza covered in onions, mushrooms, and meat, so I ordered a basic pepperoni pizza and her favorite breadsticks.

"So, are you getting excited about Christmas?" I asked, taking a drink of water to wash down my bite.

She shrugged and lifted the pizza to her mouth. It looked like she wanted to say something, then decided at the last minute not to.

"I can't wait for Christmas Eve," I continued. "You know, when Santa comes down the chimney and delivers presents." I raised my eyebrows and grinned like a goofball.

"But you don't have a chimney," she said thoughtfully, looking around the house.

Shit. She was right.

"Oh, um, yeah, I don't. But it's okay because Santa uses his magic to make them appear—remember, like in the movie we just watched?"

She frowned for a minute, and I could tell that she was trying to recall it, but in all fairness, we'd watched seven different movies today alone.

"Okay." She shrugged again and went back to eating.

She was on Christmas break this week, so I needed to come up with some things for her and Sunny to do besides watch movies. I knew Sunny was good at planning their days together, but I still felt like maybe I should provide some guidance as Sophie's parent. Calling myself her dad felt weird because I wasn't, but *guardian* sounded so cold. I was more than just her fun uncle, but I had no idea what to call it.

"Did you give any thought to what you want to ask Santa for this year for Christmas?"

She looked up at me and shook her head.

"You know you can ask for anything, right? His elves make *all* of the toys, so if there's something you want, I bet we can ask for it and see if he can deliver."

"I don't want anything."

My heart sank, and I dropped my slice of pizza onto the plate. I felt the anxiety crawl over me and wished I knew what to do. *Emily would know what to do.*

We kept eating, neither of us bothering to speak.

Finally, when we were done, I cleared our plates and put the rest in the fridge for lunch tomorrow for Sophie and Sunny.

Sophie went back to the couch and curled up with her blanket, ready to binge-watch more Christmas movies.

Suddenly, I had a spark of inspiration.

"Go get your shoes on," I said excitedly, grabbing the remote and turning the TV off.

"Why? Where are we going?" She got up and did what I asked anyway.

"We're going shopping!"

Her face lit up a little bit as she scurried down the hall and grabbed her shoes. I rushed to my bedroom and pulled a hoodie over the t-shirt and gray sweats I was wearing. It wasn't like I was trying to impress anyone, so why not be comfortable?

Once she was ready, I grabbed my phone and keys and locked the door behind us.

Going to Waldon's reminded me of Emily, and I secretly wished I would run into her there. Not that I wouldn't see her tomorrow at work, but this would be different.

I got a shopping cart and loaded Sophie into the back since she was too big to fit in the front. She seemed nervous with everyone around us, but once we got to the toy section, she relaxed.

We were busy checking out the different Baby Alive and Barbie toys when I heard someone approach us.

"I would go with the camper trailer," Sunny said, nodding to where I was focused.

"Hey," I smiled and turned to her. "What are you doing here?"

She patted the hand art that was hanging on her arm.

"Finishing the last of my Christmas shopping. You guys?" She leaned past me and waved at Sophie.

"Same. I figured it would be better just to bring her in and let her pick out what she wanted. We're running out of time for surprises," I muttered under my breath.

"Ahh." She nodded and smiled. "Well, if I may offer a suggestion, I would go with some sort of Barbie house. She really enjoys it when we play with the few she has. A little house or some clothes would be fun for her."

I looked at the shelf in front of us and pointed at the giant Barbie house.

"What about that one?"

Her eyes widened, and she tried to hide a nervous cough behind her fist.

"That is probably every little girl's dream toy," she said quietly. "But I'm not sure that you've noticed the price."

I glanced down and tried to see the tag, but it was hidden by the giant box hanging over the shelf. I checked on Sophie, who was playing with one of the Baby Alive dolls she'd picked from the shelf behind us, and then squatted to see the price.

It was regularly $300 but was on sale for $250. I didn't know much about toys, but I had to admit that even I felt excited to play with the house. It was three stories and had furniture in every room, plus other cool functions. The cost wasn't a factor, but I didn't want Sophie to see me buying it because this would make a great surprise gift from Santa.

"Thanks, I'll be sure to grab that one." I smiled warmly. I didn't want to sound like some rich douchebag who wasn't worried about the cost.

"Can we buy presents for Gracelyn and Penelope?" Sophie asked, startling me.

"Sure," I said. "Did you have something in mind that you wanted to get?"

"No, but I heard Ms. Evans say we should buy presents for our family. Aren't they our family?"

I felt the tension build in my neck as I thought about how to answer that.

"The magic of Christmas is buying gifts for people we care about and picking something that we think they would *love*," Sunny offered, standing next to Sophie in the cart.

"I care about Gracelyn, and Penelope, and Emily, and their Nana, and Uncle Jackson, and you." She smiled and lifted her chin proudly.

"Well, then, it looks like we have more shopping to do." I winked at Sophie, though I felt a bit overwhelmed trying to pick gifts for people I didn't know well enough. Okay—the problem wasn't with how well I knew them; it was that I'd never had to shop for people in my life and had no clue what I was doing.

Sunny smiled again as if noticing the panic that must've been written on my face.

"You have such a big heart, Sophie. I think they would really appreciate your thoughtfulness."

Sophie smiled back, and I felt like I was going to crumble inside.

"I can help you pick some things for them if you'd like," Sunny offered.

"Oh no, that's okay. I don't want to keep you from your own shopping."

"It's not a problem. I'm almost done anyway. Plus, I have a gift for knowing exactly what to get someone."

"Are you sure? I don't want to take advantage."

"It's fine, really." She leaned in and gently pinched Sophie's cheeks. "Let's go shopping!"

I followed her down the aisles and listened as she pointed out different things that Emily's girls would like. I added them to the extra cart we had to get and didn't worry about how much I was spending.

We had gifts for Sophie that Sunny helped pick out, as well as for Ms. Evans, Gracelyn, Penelope, and the boy at school that Sophie already had a crush on. I was ready to lose my shit until Sunny informed me that it was super innocent and that I had nothing to worry about.

"Alright, who else do we have to shop for?" Sunny asked as we reached the end of the electronics aisle. She'd recommended some new headphones for Penelope. There were a lot of options to choose from, but Sunny showed me the ones she was currently using and swore by that brand. Hers were already worn out and needed to be replaced because she used them that often, which showed how good they were.

"Nana and Emily," Sophie announced before yawning.

I glanced at my watch, noticing it was already after eight and getting close to her bedtime. We were so close to being done that I didn't want to stop and lose Sunny's help.

"Any ideas for them?" I asked desperately hoping she had some.

"Hmmm," she sighed as she thought about it. "Megan loves anything True Crime or mystery. She also loves hosting game nights every month at her house. Maybe a new serving platter? Or—"

Suddenly she stopped talking and ran down another aisle as I followed behind her, trying to pull two heavy shopping carts with me.

"This!" she exclaimed. "This is the perfect gift for Megan!"

She held up a murder-mystery board game and handed it to me.

I smiled and put it in the shopping cart.

"Done."

She pulled her eyebrows together for a moment and reconsidered.

"There's also a new book out that she would really enjoy as well. I don't know which one would be better." Her mouth pulled to the side in frustration.

"Let's grab the book; I'll get both for her."

She led the way, and we got the last copy on the shelf.

"Alright, so that leaves Emily." Of course, the one who I wanted to make sure I got something super special for but had no idea what that was.

Her phone dinged in her pocket, distracting her for a few before she replied to me.

"For Emily, there are a lot of options I can give you, but it depends on how personal you want to get with the gift."

I could hear what she was hinting at and was thankful that she didn't spell it out in front of Sophie.

"For a friend, I would look at scented candles. She enjoys vanilla and lavender scents the most and lights them when she's soaking in a bath. You could also get her some pampering products for the bath; she would love those. She likes big, fluffy blankets, coffee mugs with cute sayings, sweet wine, and sexy shoes. But if you're looking for something more personal, they sell these chocolate truffles at Sugarplum Sweets that she's obsessed with. They sell out quickly, but sometimes they will take special orders right before Christmas."

I opened my phone and made a note with all the items she mentioned, listing truffles in all capital letters.

"Thank you, Sunny. You've been more than helpful."

"Not a problem at all."

"I guess I'll finish the rest later. It's getting late, and I need to get this one to bed."

"Sounds good. I'll see you in the morning, cutie patootie," she said to Sophie.

I smiled and turned toward the registers, ready to check out.

"Oh!" Sunny blurted out, spinning around to catch us. "Did you get wrapping paper and tape?"

I tried to keep the stupid look off my face but failed.

"Nope." I cringed, knowing that I would be responsible for wrapping all of these gifts. I couldn't remember the last time I wrapped something, let alone Christmas presents.

"Come on," she laughed, pulling the cart filled with stuff in it while I followed behind her with the cart Sophie was slowly falling asleep in.

There was an entire aisle filled with nothing but rows and rows of wrapping paper, gift bags, tissue paper, ribbons, name tags, and other supplies I never knew I needed.

Sunny helped me pick some of the heavier-weight wrapping paper with Christmas designs and then made sure that I would have enough for everything I needed to wrap. I bought a new pair of scissors and what felt like twenty rolls of scotch tape. I was about to add rolls of ribbon to the cart, but Sunny assured me I didn't need it. Instead, I grabbed a couple of packs of name tags and called it good. That was more than enough Christmas shopping for one night.

Twenty
Emily

When I walked into the office Monday morning, nothing could have prepared me for what I was about to see.

Jackson was standing at the conference table with rolls of wrapping paper strewn about, rolling off the side and onto the floor. Packages of tape scattered around on top of it, as well as a mess of press-on bows that looked like they exploded out of the bag.

I covered my mouth and tried to stifle a laugh, but when he turned around, decked out in a thousand-dollar suit, and a glittery pink bow stuck to his head, I couldn't hold it in anymore.

He dropped the scissors in his hand and abandoned the gift he was attempting to wrap.

Off in the corner of the table was a pile of gifts that were *wrapped* though there were spots where he'd run short on paper and left a gap that wasn't covered. I could tell that some of the gifts were odd shapes and that he'd tried to wrap them the best he could but failed.

"What in the world happened in here?" I asked, stepping over a few bows in my stiletto heels.

I took off my coat and hung it on the coat rack next to my purse since I didn't trust it wouldn't get lost in the disaster that used to be my desk.

"I, um," he ran a hand through his hair, "was wrapping presents."

I walked over and stood beside him, hands on my hips as his eyes trailed over the tight black leather skirt I was wearing. I'd felt festive this morning but, at the last minute, decided that I wanted to look sexy instead. It wasn't that I wanted to tease Jackson with something he couldn't have, but I also loved knowing that he at least wanted me. It had been so long since I'd felt the chemistry we shared.

"Okay...."

He rubbed his lips together and stared at the mess with me.

I covered my mouth again, desperately trying not to laugh at him.

"It's fine; you can laugh," he muttered. "I have no clue what I'm doing here, obviously."

I turned to face him and smiled warmly.

"Well, lucky for you, I am the queen of gift wrapping. I can help you with this if you'd like."

I walked over to the table and examined what I had to work with.

"You don't have to do that."

"I don't mind," I insisted, hating how the vibe between us had already changed. "Besides, we're done with the festival and holiday party, so I don't have anything to work on until you give me another assignment. Plus, you're also taking up my desk space, so it helps me to help you." I winked to let him know that I was just kidding.

"Alright, if you're sure."

I could feel his hesitation and wanted to do something to ease his mind, but it was hard to do without crossing the line. Things needed to stay platonic, and that meant I needed to watch how I acted.

He gave me the rundown of what he had already attempted to wrap and then showed me the stuff he still needed to finish. Most of it was for Sophie, but I was pleasantly surprised to find that he'd also gotten something for her teacher, Sunny, and a little boy in her class whom he grumbled about her having a crush on.

We cleared the table and set up stations so I could show him how to wrap a gift. It felt like something he should already know, but then I remembered that he said he used to pay his assistant to handle his shopping, so I imagined he had her take care of the rest as well.

I smiled when I saw the collection of toys he'd picked for Sophie.

"She's going to love this doll," I said, holding up the Baby Alive. "Gracelyn has the same one and never lets go of it."

"Thanks," he said shyly. "She picked that one out herself."

"She did?"

"Yeah, I was struggling to get her to tell me what she wanted, so I gave up and took her to Waldon's. She picked the baby doll and some of the accessories that went with it."

I looked around at the other stuff and tilted my head. As if picking up on my confusion, he answered for me.

"We ran into Sunny while we were there, and she gave me some ideas for stuff Sophie would like. I went back this morning to get the stuff from Santa."

"She's going to love all of it."

"I really hope so." He looked around at the mountains of toys. "Do you think I overdid it? Should I have only gotten a few gifts? I had no idea how much to spend or if there was a certain number—"

"You did great," I assured him before he could keep talking himself out of it. "There's no limit on how much to spend or how many gifts to buy. As long as it's something you want to give her and have the money for it, that's all that matters."

He smiled and sat down in the chair across from me. The table was divided to give each of us plenty of space to wrap gifts without getting in each other's way. I made sure he had scissors, tape, and some name tags to get us started, then tackled the easy ones first.

"Okay," I said, feeling like I was a teacher. "The easiest way to make sure you have plenty of paper is to line up the box in the middle and then pull the edge around until it's fully covered. Then you can either mark the spot you need to cut or if you don't want to do that, you can just start cutting it."

I positioned the box where I needed it and began to slide the scissors over the paper, feeling satisfied as it cut through it. Jackson followed my lead, frowning and chewing his lower lip as he concentrated.

I looked away and focused on the next step to keep myself from getting distracted.

"Alright. Now that we have our paper cut to the right size, we need to tape it. First, we're going to turn the box upside down, so the back of it is facing us." I worked as I talked, making sure to go slow enough for him to keep up. "Next, we're going to put the box in the middle of the paper and then pull the long side over and secure it with a piece of tape. After that, we'll bring the other side over and tape it to the paper."

"Like this?" he asked, showing me his box.

"Perfect!"

I could see some of the tension lift from his shoulders as he pulled the package back in front of him.

"Okay, now we need to deal with the ends. Since we put the box in the middle of the paper, there should be equal space left on the top and bottom. You can pick which side you start with, but we're going to press the paper down here." I looked over to make sure he could see what I was doing. "Then we're going to fold the sides in and use our nails to create a crease line. Once you have the other side done, then we'll lift the last piece and fold it over the others and tape it right here."

He was attentive as he watched, and I suddenly felt self-conscious about how intently he was studying me.

"Then do the same thing on the other side." My voice was quieter than I expected, but I ignored it, along with the butterflies that started swarming in my stomach.

Jackson finished wrapping his gift at the same time I finished mine, then lifted it in the air to examine it before showing me.

"It looks great."

"Thank you." He grinned a toothy smile, and my heart fluttered. *Stupid heart*.

"And thank you for taking the time to show me. I know that's not in your job title, but I really do appreciate it. As you know, this is something I would have hired someone else to do for me, but I honestly enjoyed it once I learned an easier way to do it."

I laughed and felt some of the awkwardness between us dissipate.

We spent the morning wrapping the rest of the gifts, and I laughed when I saw the Barbie house he picked for Sophie from Santa and told him that I'd recently gotten the same one for Gracelyn. After I got my very generous holiday bonus, I'd snuck out to the store while my mom was watching the girls and picked out a few things that hadn't been on their list. I knew that Jackson had already purchased stuff for them as well, but this was different. While I didn't want to spoil them rotten, I also wanted to make this Christmas as special as possible since it was their first one without their dad.

We were just about done when I spotted another bag in the corner. I got up and walked over to grab it when Jackson rushed over and stood in front of me.

"No!"

I lifted my hands in surprise.

"Sorry, I just assumed it was more gifts to wrap," I apologized.

"It is," he said slowly, his body frustratingly close to mine, where I could feel the heat coming off of it.

"Okay...."

"They're gifts for you, your girls, and your mom."

My head whipped up to look at him.

"What?" I breathed out.

He nodded, his grey eyes finding mine.

"Jackson, you didn't need to—"

He lifted a finger to my lips and silenced me.

"I know I didn't need to. I wanted to. And Sophie wanted to. She was the one who brought it up."

I exhaled heavily as he lowered his finger but didn't make any effort to move away from me. I desperately wanted to reach out and touch him. To pull him to me and kiss him. But I couldn't, and I had to remember that.

"I um… I should get to work," I said awkwardly. It wasn't like I had anything to do until he gave me an assignment, but it sounded like a good excuse to distance myself from him physically.

I stepped away, making sure I took my heart with me before it could get crushed.

Twenty-One
Jackson

I was beyond thankful to Emily for helping me this morning, and I struggled with keeping my distance from her. It was hard. She was like a magnet, and I felt constantly pulled in her direction.

This week was short with Christmas Eve being on a Friday. I had asked Bea to send out a notice to the staff that we would be closing at noon on Thursday to give everyone more time to spend with their family. It felt good to do something nice for the employees, and I was surprisingly caught up on the contracts I had to send out before Christmas, which meant that this week would be easy.

It also meant that I would have even more time on my hands with nothing to do but think about Emily and all the ways I couldn't touch her.

Given that I had to wait for the contracts to be approved before I could start on those projects, I also didn't have any work to give Emily. If she hadn't asked that we stop our flirting and keep things professional between us, I would have a thousand things we could do to occupy our time. But that wasn't the case, and now I was stuck trying to figure out how to share the space with her when neither of us had anything to do.

She was sitting at the conference table that was now cleaned up, and all wrapping supplies were neatly organized at the other end. I noticed her face light up and knew she must have just read the email from Bea to the staff about closing early on Thursday.

Before she could say anything, I got up and put my coat on.

"I'm going to head out for a few and take the gifts to my house before Sunny and Sophie get back."

She looked up and glanced at me and then at the huge pile I had to take.

"Do you want some help?"

I debated on my answer for a few because while I wanted to say hell yes, I knew there were ulterior motives for taking Emily to my house—none of which I could act on.

"Umm."

"I don't mind unless you don't want me to."

I shook my head quickly and waved my hand.

"No, it's fine. I appreciate the help."

She smiled and walked over to grab a handful of the bags we'd been able to fill with the smaller wrapped gifts.

I caught sight of her tight skirt and tall heels and wondered if maybe I should have her stay here instead. I didn't want to risk her falling and breaking her neck while trying to help me get these back to my house.

But then she strutted past me with all the confidence in the world, and I knew she wasn't the one I needed to worry about. I'd be lucky not to trip over my own tongue as I followed behind her and checked out the way her ass looked in the tight leather wrapped around it.

A few trips later, we'd packed my car full—the back seat, trunk, and a few boxes that sat on Emily's lap, and headed to my house.

I knew Sunny had taken Sophie to the museum for a special Santa breakfast and some Christmas activities, but I didn't know how long they'd be there. I wanted to make sure that I got the majority of the gifts from Santa hidden in my office before they got back. I was pretty new to the whole *parent thing*, but I knew enough to stay out of sight until after she went to bed on Christmas Eve.

I pulled into the garage and turned off the car before rushing to open Emily's door and taking the boxes from her so that she could get out. I balanced them in one arm while I fumbled with opening the door. Once open, I stepped to the side and held it as Emily walked past me with a handful of packages she'd grabbed from the back seat.

"Where would you like these?" she asked, stopping in the kitchen and looking around.

She'd been to my house the day she came to help Sophie find Mr. Floppsy and do her hair, but we'd been in a rush, so I didn't get the chance to give her a tour of it.

"My office," I said behind the stack I was carrying. "Down the hall, first door on the left."

I heard her footsteps on the tile in the kitchen until they disappeared into the carpet. I followed her, knowing the way, and waited until I heard the office door open before I went any further. The last thing I wanted to do was plow into her by accident.

"Anywhere in particular?" she asked, stepping to the side so I could come in.

"By the table is fine."

I set mine down on the floor next to it and smiled as she carefully set hers on top.

We made a few more trips and brought in the rest, making my office look like Santa's workshop.

"I didn't get a good look at it before we started, but I could swear that I saw a desk in here somewhere," Emily joked, looking around the room.

"Umm... Yeah. I guess I should have given you the tour before we got started," I laughed. "Thanks again for the help. I failed to realize just how much stuff I had."

"So," Emily said nervously, wringing her hands together in front of her. "I have something that I want to ask, and I don't know if it's my place."

"Okay," I said easily, leaning against what looked like the corner of my desk and folding my arms over my chest.

"I was wondering if it was okay if the girls and I could take Sophie for a few hours one night this week."

I peered at her, my curiosity getting the best of me.

"The girls and I have this tradition that we started with Mark where we would separate into teams and buy for the others. That way, we could surprise them, but the girls got to be included and pick out their own gifts that they wanted to get for everyone. Then we would swap kids and shop for the others. It was a nice way of making sure everyone had a chance to buy something without the surprise of it being ruined."

"So you want to take Sophie to..." My mind failed to comprehend what she was saying as my eyes focused on how her lips moved as she spoke.

"We'd like to take her shopping to buy something for you for Christmas."

Her eyes lit up as she said it, and I felt a tightness in my heart.

"Oh, no, thank you, but that's not necessary."

Aside from the gift that Cammy would send every year, I couldn't remember the last time anyone bought me something for the holiday. It never bothered me, probably because I was able to buy myself whatever I wanted, whenever I wanted, but it always felt special with the little things Cammy would get me. I knew she tried to stretch her dollar as far as she could while supporting herself and Sophie, and I always hated how she refused my help.

She scrunched her face, and I knew she was going to keep pushing it.

"I know you may not think that you need anything for Christmas but imagine how Sophie might feel if she's the only one opening gifts that day. I think it would mean a lot to her if she were able to buy you something and watch as you open it."

I nodded and then hung my head. She was right.

"Alright," I smiled and exhaled heavily. "Thank you for being so considerate and offering to do that for us."

"My pleasure."

Speaking of pleasure…

I pushed away from the desk and cleared my throat.

"Why don't I give you a tour of the house?" I offered, pulling my thoughts away from the bulge growing in my pants.

I had no idea if she even cared to see the house, but I needed to get out of this room and do something to distract me.

She nodded and followed as I led her out the door and down the hallway. I showed her the guest bedroom, Sophie's room, the guest bathroom, and the laundry room before we finally landed at my room. If I thought being alone with her in my office was hard, I didn't think about how worse it would be here.

I walked in and stepped to the side as she looked around, taking in the tall windows facing the woods and the massive king-sized bed that had been made that morning before I left. There wasn't much in the room other than furniture, and a couple of paintings hung neatly on the cream-colored walls.

She peeked into the bathroom and gasped when she saw the double vanity and large soaking tub that had a frosted window that allowed you to look out without anyone being able to see in.

"Your house is gorgeous," she commented, joining me in the middle of the room.

I toed the edge of the rug under the bed and kept from looking at her.

"Thank you."

The chemistry between us sizzled, and I knew she could feel it too by the way her cheeks flushed and her body leaned into mine. I clenched my hands into fists at my side, trying to keep from reaching out to touch her.

"Emily," I breathed out in warning. My resolve was wearing thin.

Before I could say anything more, she was in my arms with hers wrapped around my neck and her lips pressed against mine.

Our kiss was urgent, passionate, and more than just something that happened between friends. I wanted Emily more than anything and hated that I couldn't have her.

The deeper she kissed me, the harder I got. I reached down and lifted her to my waist, loving how she locked her legs behind me as I grabbed her ass.

I walked us the few steps back to my bed and debated on whether to lay her down on it. I didn't want to take advantage of the situation, but when she whimpered about how much she wanted me, I knew we didn't have any fight left in us.

I tossed her gently, enjoying the sound as she giggled and shimmied up the bed while I climbed up beside her.

"Oh, I should take my shoes off," she said, reaching down to remove them.

"Don't," I rushed out, placing my hand on hers to stop her. "They're so fucking sexy, I want to see you in them and nothing but them."

She blushed again and laid back as I leaned down and kissed the top of her foot, then trailed my tongue slowly up her leg until I reached the hem of her skirt. It was super tight, which would make it hard to get access to her, but I also loved that it was such a fucking sexy barrier.

I adjusted so I was lying beside her and skimmed my fingers up the inside of her thigh as she willingly parted her legs as much as she could with the fabric restricting her.

My fingers brushed against the lace fabric of her panties, and I groaned as loud as she did when I pushed them to the side. I could feel the strain of my erection against the zipper of my pants but tried to ignore it as I gently caressed her.

Her breathing got heavier as I took my time teasing her before sliding a finger in between her folds. She gasped at the intrusion and arched her back off of the bed. She was already so wet that there was no resistance when I slid another one in and pumped them.

I kept the rhythm she seemed to like and focused on how her body was reacting. I could tell she was getting close when I started rubbing her clit with my thumb and her legs tightened against me. Instead of watching my hand as it disappeared under her skirt, I focused on the way her lips parted and how her face revealed the pleasure she was feeling as I sent her over the edge.

She cried out, clenching her thighs tightly against my hand to keep it in place as I drew out the last of her orgasm with my fingers. Once she was done, she panted heavily and let her legs fall to the side as much as the skirt would allow. I pulled my hand free and leaned down to kiss her when I heard the chime of the alarm when the front door opened.

I jumped off of the bed, startling her.

"What's wrong?" she asked, scooting down quickly as she adjusted her clothes.

"Sunny and Sophie are back."

Her eyes widened as she stood beside me and pulled her skirt down.

I reached down and tried to adjust myself so no one saw my bulging erection.

Sunny didn't know we were there since I'd parked in the garage and I didn't want to scare her.

"Follow my lead," I whispered to Emily, knowing that we didn't have much time if I was going to pull this off.

She nodded and chewed her lip nervously before I reached up and popped it free.

"So, that's the guest bathroom, and then the laundry room is at the end," I said loudly, making sure it was enough for Sunny to hear.

Emily and I had moved out into the hallway so it would look like I was giving her a proper tour and not fingering her on my bed as I had been.

"Wow, that's beautiful. I love the organization in here," Emily replied loudly before I pulled the door to the laundry room closed.

We walked a few steps down the hallway before Sophie rounded the corner and came running at us.

"Uncle Jackson! What are you doing here?" she asked, wrapping her arms around my neck as I knelt down to pick her up.

"I brought Emily by to drop some stuff off and decided to show her the house since she didn't get to see it the last time she was here."

"Hi, Emily." Sophie waved, still clinging to me like a monkey.

Sunny came down the hallway a few minutes later with a smug smile, like she knew exactly what Emily and I had been doing.

"Hey, Sunny," I said casually, as if I just randomly showed up during the week when I was supposed to be at work.

"Hi." Her grin spread even wider when she looked at Emily and said hi.

"Well, we didn't mean to interrupt your guys' day," I said, nodding to Sunny and Sophie after I set her down. "We'd better get back to work."

"Do you have to go back already?" Sophie pouted.

I squatted in front of her again, waiting for her to look at me.

"I'm sorry, Pumpkin. But I promise we'll play as soon as I get home today. Okay?"

She nodded, but I could tell she was still disappointed.

"Okay."

"Is something else bothering you?" I asked, squatting down in front of her.

She waited a few minutes and then looked up at Emily before answering.

"I wanted Emily to stay with us."

I glanced behind me and saw the way she was looking at Sophie. She squatted beside me and took Sophie's hand in hers.

"I would love to spend some time with you, Sophie. But your Uncle is right; we have to get back to work."

I could see the tears in Sophie's eyes as she tried to blink them away.

"But I talked to him earlier, and he said it would be alright if you came shopping with my girls and me one night this week. Would you like to do that?"

Her little face lit up as she smiled and nodded.

"Well, then, it's a date. I'll talk to your uncle and see what day works best for you guys. Maybe we can have dinner before we go shopping."

It didn't seem possible, but Sophie's grin stretched even further. She gave Emily a big hug before running off to the living room with Sunny.

"You ready to go?" Emily asked as we followed them out.

In more ways than one.

Twenty-Two
Emily

The tension between us was palpable as we drove back to the office. I could tell that Jackson was just as flustered by almost getting caught as I was. The only difference was that my embarrassment came with a whopping side of guilt for failing to keep my word to Penelope that I wasn't going to start anything with anyone until she and Gracelyn were ready.

When we got back to the office, Jackson asked me to help Bea with a project which kept me tied up until five, when we all left for the day. I walked back to the office to grab my stuff and noticed a frown on Jackson's face.

"What's wrong?" I asked, pulling my coat on.

"My attorney wants to meet tonight to discuss the final things we need to handle with my sister's will. I was trying to see if Sunny could stay late tonight, but she already has another family she's sitting for. If I don't meet with him tonight, we won't be able to until after the new year because he's leaving for Hawaii tomorrow morning."

"Why don't I take her tonight? We wanted to go shopping with her anyway," I shrugged.

He looked up from his phone, the frown slowly fading.

"Are you sure?"

I nodded.

"I can follow you home and pick her up. I'll let my mom know about the change in plans and have her get the girls ready to go. Do you mind if we take her out to dinner too?"

He leaned back in his chair and shoved a hand through his short hair.

"You have no idea how much you're saving me right now. I don't want to deal with my sister's stuff any longer than I have to. It breaks my heart, and I feel like I'm losing her all over again every time I have to handle her estate. Thank you, and I'll pay for your guys' dinner tonight."

"No," I said sharply, holding my hand up to stop him as he pulled his wallet out and started reaching inside. "Thank you, but I've got it."

"Emily," he warned, tilting his head to the side. "I appreciate you helping me. The least I can do is treat for dinner."

"And I appreciate the offer," I replied, planting my hands on my hips. 'But we want to take Sophie out. It's our pleasure."

"Alright," he sighed and stood up, gathering his stuff so we could get going.

On the drive to his house, I called my mother on speakerphone and let her know about the change in plans. The girls squealed loudly in the background when she told them we were going to dinner and then out shopping with Sophie. I loved how much they adored her and felt this strange pull on my heart.

When we got there, I tried to push the memories of this afternoon in his bedroom as far away as possible. My body had felt alive under his touch, and now I craved more of it, even though I knew it couldn't happen.

Sophie and Sunny were playing Barbies until Jackson told her the plans, and she got up and ran over to hug me. Sunny smiled brightly, watching the interaction.

I stood up and waited for Jackson to help Sophie get her stuff ready.

"It's nice of you to take her shopping," Sunny said warmly.

"Thanks. I wanted to make sure Jackson had something to open for Christmas too." Not that I hadn't already bought a few gifts for him and Sophie, though I didn't need to tell Sunny that.

"It has to be hard not having a family to celebrate the holidays with."

I nodded, feeling the lump forming in my throat.

"Are Gracelyn and Penelope excited for Christmas?"

"I think so, but I can tell it doesn't feel the same for them. I'm trying to make it as special as I can, but I can't stop feeling like I'm failing."

Sunny smiled sadly, knowing our story and that this was the first year without Mark. She was a lot younger than me but still wise for her age and had such an incredible gift for knowing what people needed, even if they didn't realize it themselves.

"When we lost my dad..." she said quietly, looking out the window to watch the snow fall as she spoke. "My mom didn't know what to do. The holidays were hard, and even though we all tried to be happy for each other, we were devastated not to have him there with us. That night, I caught my mom crying in the kitchen as she was cleaning up dinner.

It was the first time I'd seen her cry, and it broke me."

I felt my eyes get teary and knew that my girls would probably feel the same way if they saw me break down the way that I wanted to.

She reached over and gently touched my arm to get my attention.

"It broke me in the best way possible. It showed me that I didn't have to pretend to be strong anymore. We could be sad together and cry together and mourn him together. After that, everything felt so much lighter because we weren't treading lightly to keep from upsetting each other. It was still hard not having my dad there, but the weight that was lifted from trying to pretend that we weren't hurting was immense."

"I'm sorry about your dad," I whispered, not trusting my voice not to betray me and show my emotion.

"I don't want to overstep, but maybe if the girls still seem like they're struggling with the holiday without their dad, try to find a way to include him and encourage them to talk about him. And cry. Whatever they need. Whatever you all need. It can be something as simple as picking a special ornament for him that you guys put on the tree every year to remember him. Or tell your favorite stories about him. But whatever you do, give yourself some grace, Emily. You're doing an amazing job, and I can't begin to imagine what it feels like for you right now."

I nodded and sucked in a deep breath.

Before we could say anything more, Jackson and Sophie came back. His eyes narrowed as he looked between Sunny and me, wondering why I suddenly looked upset. I shook my head and forced a smile at Sophie, who looked adorable in her furry boots, leggings, and a Christmas sweater that looked soft and cozy.

"Are you ready?" I asked, holding my hand out for hers.

"I am!"

"Let me know when you're done, and I'll bring her back. We'll probably be gone for a few hours with dinner and shopping, but I'll have my cell if you need me."

"Sounds good, thank you. He's meeting me here, so you're welcome to bring her back whenever you're ready. I don't expect this to take too long, but I've been wrong before."

We said goodbye to Sunny, and then Jackson helped me load Sophie's booster seat into my SUV. It felt weird to take her without him coming with us, but I was also super excited to spend time with her on our own. She waved to him as we drove off, and my heart did another weird thing where it felt like it grew bigger than it could handle.

Twenty-Three
Emily

My mom and I watched as the girls giggled and ate their pizza while talking about something funny that had happened to Gracelyn at school. It warmed my heart to see them bonding. I wanted to talk to them about finding an ornament to put on the tree for their dad this year, but my nerves were a jumbled mess, and I was struggling with how to bring it up. I hadn't even talked to my mom about it yet, so I was literally on my own.

Once they were done, we cleaned up the mess and wiped the younger girls down with a few baby wipes. Thankfully I always kept a small pack in my purse for these occasions.

"What are you going to buy your uncle?" Gracelyn asked Sophie.

She tapped her chin with her finger while she thought about it.

"A puppy!" she exclaimed happily.

I laughed and shook my head.

"Is that what Uncle Jackson wants or what Sophie wants?" I asked with an arched brow.

She blushed and covered her cute little face with her hands.

"Me!"

"You silly girl," I laughed. My girls were getting restless, and I knew it was now or never. I cleared my throat and waited a few seconds to get the courage that I needed.

"So, I wanted to talk to you two for a moment before we go shopping," I said gently. My mom's eyes narrowed slightly, likely wondering what I was up to.

"I, um, I know that this year has been hard without your dad." I swallowed hard and noticed how their little bodies stiffened at the mention of him.

"I think we should get something to honor him this year. Maybe a special ornament that we put on the tree? Or if you guys have other ideas, I would love to hear them."

My voice cracked at the end, and I blinked away the tears.

"I would like that," Penelope said, grabbing my attention. When I looked at her, I saw the way her eyes were watering too.

"Me too," Gracelyn added more enthusiastically than any of us.

"Okay, we'll be sure to look tonight while we're shopping." I looked over and noticed how sad Sophie had gotten and had completely overlooked the fact that she was also spending her first Christmas without her mom.

I reached over and gently squeezed her hand.

"Sophie, would you like to look for an ornament or something special to remember your mom?"

She nodded and then burst into tears. I scooted over and scooped her into my arms, hugging her as she cried.

By the time we got to the store, we all had red eyes— including my mom—and looked like one of the vampires from the Twilight movie. But after crying for a bit, we all felt better, and the mood seemed to have shifted. Sunny might have been onto something after all, and I made a note to make sure I stopped trying to hide my grief from the girls. While I thought I was doing them a favor by being strong, I now realized that they were simply following my lead and hiding their own.

We made our first stop at the Christmas ornaments and took our time looking through them. The girls decided on one with a guy on a boat, about to fall in as he tried to reel in a fish. It was adorable and totally reminded us of Mark, and the time he almost went deep sea swimming when his catch nearly pulled him overboard.

Sophie looked through the ornaments but seemed to struggle with finding one she liked. I sent the girls with my mom to look at some decorations while I gave Sophie some time to keep looking. I didn't want her to feel rushed or overwhelmed.

I was looking at a beautiful ornament of a mother holding her baby when I felt Sophie's eyes on me. I held it out and showed it to her.

She smiled and then started crying again. I bent down and held her to me as her little body shook with sadness.

"It's okay, honey," I whispered. "It's okay."

She pulled back and wiped her face with the sleeves of her sweater.

"I miss my mommy."

"I know, sweet girl. I'm so sorry."

We put the ornament in the top of the cart with the one my girls picked for Mark. I arranged my coat to protect them, so they didn't break before we got them home.

"Alright," I said once we were situated. "Do you know what you want to get your uncle?"

She smiled, shook her head, and then reached up and held my hand as we walked around the store together.

We found my mom and the girls in the clothing section, so we ventured on to the men's. I felt like I had a good feel for Jackson and what he might like, but then again, I hadn't known him long enough.

I kept hold of Sophie's hand as we browsed through a few racks of t-shirts. Jackson didn't strike me as the kind of guy to wear t-shirts, but maybe that was exactly what he needed. He was forty-two, not eighty.

Sophie and I looked through the graphic tees and added a handful to the cart. She found some that made her laugh, and I couldn't help but want to see more of it. Next, we went to the gloves and hat section, and I looked at a few pairs of leather gloves. I hadn't seen him wear any, so I wasn't sure if he had some. I held up a brown and black pair and waited for Sophie to pick.

She decided on the black ones, so I added them to the cart along with a scarf that I thought would look great on him too. It was funny that I felt totally comfortable shopping for him as if I were his girlfriend. It felt comforting and disturbing at the same time.

An hour later, we had the shopping cart filled and were ready to check out when my mom remembered she needed to get a dessert to take to the monthly game night she had with some of her friends. We got in line and waited for her while the people ahead of us slowly trickled through. Only a handful of cashiers were working, which seemed odd given that it was less than a week away from Christmas, and they were swamped tonight.

Finally, my mom returned with a brownie platter, a few rolls of wrapping paper, and scotch tape that I'd forgotten to grab. We planned to take Sophie back to our house and wrap the gifts before we took her back to Jackson's, but it was getting late, and she looked tired.

I pulled out my phone and sent him a quick text message, letting him know we were finishing up. He confirmed that the lawyer had just left and offered to come to pick Sophie up to keep us from going out of our way to drop her off.

I didn't mind taking her, so I told him we would go ahead and bring her back, then made sure he knew that my girls would be with me as well. My mom had taken her car and planned to head home once we were done.

We packed up the back of the SUV, and then I covered the pile of bags with a blanket to keep it hidden until we could help Sophie wrap the gifts. I had no idea how we would manage that on such short notice, but I knew I had to try. Penelope was on ornament duty as she sat up front beside me, making sure none of our new valued treasures got damaged.

When I pulled up at Jackson's house, I felt my stomach twist with the excitement of seeing him.

Penelope guarded the ornament while I helped Sophie and Gracelyn out of the car. Jackson was standing at the front door, leaning against the frame, wearing a snug-fitting sweater and dress slacks.

As we got closer, Sophie ran over and wrapped him in a hug. The girls and I stayed behind for a few to give them time together. Jackson lifted her into his arms and then stepped back to hold the door open for us.

"Did you have a good time?" he asked her as he set her down and closed the front door.

"It was so much fun, Uncle Jackson!"

"I'm happy to hear that, Squirt."

"Did you want to show him what you got?" I asked softly and then looked up at Jackson, hoping that he wasn't going to be mad at me for having Sophie pick out an ornament for her mom. I should have asked him first and didn't think about it until we were on our way here.

She smiled as Penelope handed her the bag and gently took it out.

Jackson's face lit up and then fell when he squatted to look at it while she held it in her hands.

"It's for my mom," she said sadly, starting to cry again. "It's a mommy holding their baby."

Jackson pulled her in for a hug, and I turned away as I heard them sniffling together. I could tell he was trying to hold it together for her but was losing the battle.

He quickly wiped his eyes with his hands and then stood up with her. I tried to ignore the way his muscles bulged under his sweater. Now wasn't the time or place to be entertaining those kinds of thoughts.

"Where would you like to put it?" he asked, holding her in front of the Christmas tree.

Her beautiful blue eyes looked around until she found the perfect spot and pointed. He leaned forward as she reached out and put the ornament on the branch, making sure it was secure before she let go.

He set her down, and they looked at it together as he rested his hands on her shoulders. From behind, I could tell by the way his shoulders trembled that he was struggling right now. I nodded to my girls to go stand with Sophie as I walked over and gently touched Jackson's shoulder.

I felt the tension in his body as he looked away from me.

"Come with me for a moment," I whispered, leading him away.

He tried to keep his face turned away from me, but once we got to the hallway, I pulled him into me and held him as he started to cry. He wrapped his arms around me and hid his face in my hair as his body trembled.

I looked up to see Penelope watching us and knew that this would be another blow to her. But at that moment, I knew that Jackson needed someone to be there for him as he grieved his sister, and other than me, he didn't have anyone.

Twenty-Four

Jackson

"I'm sorry," I whispered, desperately trying to wipe my face before Emily could see I was crying.

I felt like a total moron for losing it in front of her, but after meeting with my lawyer, my emotions were high and I was missing Cammy even more.

Things had been so busy with getting Sophie situated and planning stuff at work that I hadn't allowed myself to slow down and deal with my grief. It had been building and building until I finally lost it.

"You have nothing to be sorry about," she assured me.

When I finally pulled away, I spotted Penelope watching us before she turned and went back to the living room with Gracelyn and Sophie.

"I think Penelope saw us."

"Yeah, I know." She sighed heavily, and I hated that I was causing her more problems.

"I didn't mean—"

"You didn't do anything, Jackson. I'll talk to her, but you don't need to worry about it. It's not a big deal."

I pulled my lips into a thin line and leaned my shoulder against the wall. It hadn't occurred to me that I didn't have any framed photos in the house until my lawyer mentioned the personal belongings in Cammy's home that I would need to go through soon. Since she didn't have any family other than Sophie and me, I was now in charge of doing something with the house.

It became real to me when I imagined going back and sorting through her things. The fact that my sister would never walk through those doors again or tuck Sophie into bed in her room—that broke my heart.

I'd been so focused on getting her set up here, that I hadn't realized that Sophie had another life she'd been forced to leave behind. I'd agreed to send in the next few month's mortgage payments to make sure it didn't go into foreclosure and made a note to get someone to set up a security system for me until I could get out there in January.

"Are you okay?" Emily asked after I'd been quiet for a few minutes.

"Yeah," I said on an exhale. "Between meeting with my lawyer and the beautiful ornament, it was just a lot for me today."

"I'm sorry, I should have asked first. Sunny asked me earlier about how my girls were handling their first Christmas without their dad and recommended getting something special to honor him. I didn't want Sophie to feel left out, so we asked her to pick one for her mom. But I realize now that I should have asked you first and shouldn't have assumed it was okay. Maybe you wanted to be the one to take her, or—"

"Emily, it's fine; you don't have to worry about it. I'm glad that you guys included her in that. I can't say that it's something I would have thought to do on my own, so thank you for making it special for her. I know it means a lot to her," I said, interrupting her.

I looked past her into the living room, where Sophie sat on the floor with Gracelyn and looked up at the tree. Penelope was sitting in the armchair across from them, watching her mom and me.

"I know it's probably not my place," I said quietly since we had an audience. "But do you want me to try talking to her? Maybe she'll believe there's nothing going on between us if it comes from me instead?"

She smiled sadly and shook her head.

"Thank you, but I'll talk to her when we get home." She looked down and checked her watch. "Which, we should get going; it's late."

We walked into the living room together and stood there as the girls all turned to look at us.

"We need to get going," Emily announced to her girls.

"Thank you guys for helping Sophie with her Christmas shopping," I said, looking between Gracelyn and Penelope. I wanted them to like me, which was weird because I'd never cared what anyone thought of me until now.

I walked them out to their car, letting Sophie trail beside me. Emily got her girls situated before turning to talk to me.

"So, we have stuff that Sophie needs to wrap, but we ran out of time. I was thinking, if you guys would like to, maybe you can come over for dinner tomorrow night, and then when we're done, my girls can help Sophie wrap her gifts?"

Sophie tugged at my arm excitedly as she bounced around like a little jumping bean.

"I don't want to put you guys out another night," I said, not wanting to take advantage of her hospitality.

"You're not. It's an invitation, and I know my girls would love to hang out with Ms. Sophie again. But if you already have plans, I completely understand."

"I don't have plans." I locked eyes with her, making sure she got exactly what I was saying. She was the only person who I wanted to make plans with.

"Great, then we'll see you guys tomorrow at six." She smiled and climbed into her SUV before driving away.

****

I knocked on the door and waited nervously for Emily to answer. It felt like being a teenager, going on a date for the first time.

Penelope opened the door, and I felt my anxiety lessen a little when she smiled and then moved aside to let us in.

"Hi, Penelope!" Sophie said excitedly.

Penelope wrapped her in a big hug and told her how excited she was to see her. I didn't expect anything from Penelope, so I shrugged out of my coat and hung it on the coat rack behind the door, only to be surprised when I felt her arms wrap around my waist for a quick hug before she let go and rushed off with Sophie.

I made my way to the kitchen with the bottle of wine I had brought. I remembered that Emily enjoyed sweeter ones, so I grabbed a Moscato and hoped it was good.

"Hey, do you need any help?" I asked, startling her by accident.

"Jackson!" She spun around and held her hand to her chest. "I didn't know you were here."

"Sorry. We rang the doorbell, and Penelope answered."

She frowned.

"The doorbell must be broken again because I didn't hear it."

"I can take a look at it for you if you'd like."

She turned back to the hamburger meat she was cooking in the skillet.

"You don't have to but thank you for the offer. It's on my list of things to deal with in January."

I nodded and folded my arms over my chest. I wanted to ask her about Penelope and why she was being so nice to me, but I didn't want to ruin a good thing before it started.

"Dinner smells delicious. Are you sure you don't need any help?"

"Nah, I've got it. We're having sloppy joes—I hope that's okay with you guys?"

"Of course. We're thankful for the meal."

"My girls love sloppy joes, and sometimes I forget that other people aren't fans of messy food."

"Eh, I'll buy Sophie new clothes if she ruins them. I'm not worried."

She looked at me over her shoulder as she stirred the seasoning mixture in.

"They do make this stuff called *stain remover*," she joked.

"Yeah, but laundry is overrated."

She spun around, her jaw dropping in response.

"You don't do laundry?" she asked in mock surprise.

"Nope. I pay someone to take care of it for me."

"You're kidding, right?"

I shook my head, feeling slightly embarrassed that she must think I was incapable of taking care of myself.

She laughed, and it lightened the mood.

"I wish I had someone to do the laundry for me. With three girls, it adds up quickly."

"I'll send my lady over," I offered. "She does an amazing job."

She turned the stove off and moved the skillet to another burner.

"Thank you, but I'm good. There's no way I could afford that."

"I'll pay." I shrugged, totally willing to do this for her.

"You're very generous to offer but save that money for Sophie." She patted my chest, the heat from her hand spreading through my body.

"Dinner is ready," she called to the kids in the living room. "Go wash your hands."

I helped her get the plates down and set the table while the giggling from the bathroom floated into the kitchen. I loved the sound of the girls talking and laughing together. It was as if Sophie had an extended family with Gracelyn and Penelope. This was something that I couldn't give her, just like how

Emily provided her the type of comfort Cammy used to.

Once everyone was situated, Emily passed things around the table, and we helped the girls fix their plates.

The girls took turns telling Christmas-themed knock-knock jokes while we ate, and I found myself smiling more than I had in a long time.

At one point, I was in the middle of taking a drink of my Dr. Pepper when Penelope launched a hilarious one at us, and I ended up with soda coming out of my nose. That got everyone laughing even harder.

After dinner, I helped Emily clean up in the kitchen while the girls took Sophie to Penelope's room for some top-secret gift wrapping. Once we were done, we sat down on the couch and talked about the weather because it was a lot easier than talking about what we were feeling between us.

It didn't take a genius to see how easily our families blended together. We were comfortable and got along so well that I was genuinely curious about what it would look like if this thing between Emily and I worked out. How different it would be to come here every night and call it home or to have Emily and the girls move in with me. I mean, hell, I had plenty of room for all of us with three spare bedrooms, two of which shared a jack-and-jill bathroom.

Suddenly, there was a burst of laughter that came down the hallway. Emily and I looked in that direction to see what the girls were doing. Penelope's door was still closed, so we let it be and stayed put.

"It sounds like they're having fun in there," I noted, nodding toward the room.

"They have so much fun when they're together. The girls really enjoy having Sophie around."

"*I* enjoy having the girls around." I wanted her to know that it wasn't just her company that I enjoyed but that I adored her girls as well and loved having them around.

There was a small gap between us on the couch that was just enough space to keep us from jumping each other's bones but not enough to keep me from reaching over and brushing her finger with mine.

Her breathing changed, and I could tell she felt the same thing I did. It happened every time we touched, even when we tried not to.

"In a perfect world, we would all be together, Emily," I whispered. "And not just for dinner or shopping or to help do Sophie's hair. We would be a family, which isn't something I ever saw myself having. But I want it, Emily. I want it so fucking bad."

She opened her mouth to say something, her eyes filled with emotion. But before she could speak, Penelope's door swung open, and the girls came out carrying armloads of wrapped gifts.

I looked at the pile and then turned and pinned Emily with a look, pretending to be upset.

"Those are all for me?" I asked, eyes wide and brows raised.

"Ummm," she giggled nervously and then pulled her sleeves over her hands and held them in front of her face. "Maybe?"

"Some of them are for mommy, too," Gracelyn announced.

"Nana snuck in a few more gifts last night when you were shopping with Sophie."

"What?" Emily grinned at her daughters. "That's very thoughtful of you guys. Did you separate them so we can help Jackson load theirs to take to their house?"

The three girls paused for a moment, looking at each other before looking back at us.

"What are you three up to?" Emily asked, obviously knowing her girls too well.

"We thought we could put them under our tree," Gracelyn said, pointing to where it was already overflowing with gifts.

"But then Jackson wouldn't have presents to open on Christmas day." Emily frowned, not following where they were going with this.

Sophie caught my eye and winked. I hadn't been doing this long, but I knew enough to know that she was up to no good as well.

"That's why we thought Jackson and Sophie could come here for Christmas," Penelope said, looking from her mom to me. "We would love for you guys to join us if it's okay with my mom."

I pulled back in surprise.

"Where did this come from?" Emily asked softly, leaning forward and resting her elbows on her knees.

Penelope looked down, her cheeks blushing with embarrassment.

"It was my idea."

Emily gasped quietly, but it was enough for me to hear. I knew it was as big of a shock for her as it was for me.

"Okay," she said slowly. "We can talk about it later. I don't know what Jackson had planned for Christmas with Sophie, and we wouldn't want to interfere."

"We don't have plans," Sophie volunteered proudly.

Emily turned and looked at me for help.

I shrugged, having no clue what to do or say.

"I know you guys are trying to pretend that you don't like each other," Penelope blurted out. "But I can see how much you make each other smile. I'm not going to be mad about that. We love hanging out and spending time with Sophie, and dinner was really fun tonight with Jackson here. Even if he sprayed soda all over the table out of his nose," she giggled. "Christmas is hard for all of us, and I thought maybe we could make it better if we spent it together. Tonight was fun, so maybe Christmas would be too?"

I could hear the emotion rising in her voice. Emily got up and walked over to her, pulling her in for a hug as Penelope sniffled.

A few minutes later, Penelope pulled away but stayed tucked into Emily's side as she wiped the tears from her cheeks.

"So, what do you say? Do you guys want to spend Christmas with us?" Emily asked as the other two girls clung to her other side.

I looked at the image in front of me and grinned. *My girls— all of them.*

"I would love nothing more."

Twenty-Five

Jackson

"Do you know if Sophie had any traditions she did with Cammy?" Emily asked as we waited for the popcorn to finish popping in the kitchen.

"I don't. She hasn't mentioned anything to me yet, so I keep hoping she'll tell me if she remembers anything."

"Well, it's good to start making new ones too."

"Like spending Christmas Eve in Christmas pajamas, watching movies, playing games, and eating junk food?" I asked, pointing to her reindeer PJs.

They were tight fitting which did nothing to help me keep the bulge hidden in my pants. Hers was a reindeer that had a little deer butt on her ass, and I found myself wanting to take her for a ride—literally.

My pajamas weren't any better—probably because Emily picked them out with the girls last night when we agreed that Sophie and I would spend the night tonight so we could all wake up early and open gifts together. Mine was a green onesie that resembled the Grinch, and I had to wonder who was responsible for it.

We took the bowls of popcorn to the living room and set them down on the coffee table with the other snacks. The girls were camped out on an air mattress in front of the TV, watching one of the Santa Clause movies. I couldn't tell you which one because I'd been too busy having naughty thoughts with *Prancer* sitting beside me.

Emily and I had talked about the recent conversations she'd had with Penelope, and it turned out that her change of heart had come from a conversation she had with Megan while Emily was shopping with Sophie. Penelope said that hearing her grandmother talk about how happy she'd noticed Emily had been had changed her mind about things. Megan assured her that if Emily and I got together, it would never replace Mark, just like Emily would never replace Cammy for Sophie.

Penelope was only nine but seemed to understand that I wasn't the threat she initially worried I was. With our families naturally blending together, it made it easier for everyone to see where the pieces would fall if we decided to move forward and give this a try.

When Sophie and I came over this morning, Emily took her and Gracelyn to the bathroom to do their hair, giving me time to sit and talk with Penelope. I was probably more nervous than she was, but when I remembered that she was just a scared little girl, everything else faded away, and I made sure that she knew she could trust me. We kept the serious conversation to a minimum and then spent the rest of the time seeing who could come up with better dad jokes. I mean, I guess it was in the job title that I needed to learn some, so why not start now? Although, I preferred to call them uncle jokes for now. Labels were still a hard thing for me to wrap my head around.

The night wore down, and the girls headed to bed after they each got to open one present. The girls all set up camp in

Gracelyn's room with sleeping bags and piles of pillows. After we made sure they were asleep, we brought out the gifts that I had been hiding in the garage that were from Santa.

We drank some of the milk, and Emily nibbled the cookie, which only made me hornier when I thought about eating her cookie. Then, we turned off the lights and went to her room. We hadn't talked about where I would sleep tonight, but when she led me there with her little reindeer ass shaking along the way, I wasn't about to object.

She closed the door and locked it, giving me a knowing look when she spun around.

"I've been waiting all night to get my hands on you," she purred, wrapping her arms around my neck and bringing her lips to mine.

"Same here. Those reindeer pajamas really have an effect on me." I pressed my groin against her pelvis, showing her how hard I was for her.

One thing about having sex with kids in the house was that sometimes you had to be fast. Emily and I wasted no time stripping out of our pajamas and climbing into her bed.

There were a million things that I wanted to do to her, but there wasn't time. We didn't want to risk Sophie coming to look for me if she woke up in a room she didn't recognize.

I laid beside her, my fingers already parting her wet folds and slipping inside as she gasped loudly and then moaned softly. I kissed her neck and licked along her collarbone before dipping down and pulling a hardened nipple into my mouth.

I sucked hard, gently nipping her with my teeth before taking the other one into my mouth. With two fingers pumping inside of her, I rubbed her clit with my thumb and felt the way she tightened around me.

Within minutes, she was coming hard, her pussy clenching as it spasmed.

"You're so fucking good at that," she panted.

I chuckled and pulled my hand away. I didn't have my wallet on me since I'd been wearing pajamas, so I didn't have a condom handy.

"I don't have protection," I said disappointedly as she reached over and stroked my cock.

"It's okay. I'm on the pill. Haven't been with anyone since Mark." She leaned forward and nipped my earlobe.

"I haven't been with anyone in a while either. And I get tested often, I'm clean."

"Okay, then fuck me, please," she begged.

I was about to roll over and do as she asked, but she surprised me when she climbed on top of me instead.

I held her hips and helped lower her onto my dick. She gasped as she slid down, feeling the pressure as she wrapped around the girth.

"You're huge," she moaned and closed her eyes.

Slowly she slid the rest of the way until I was fully seated inside her. I laid there and let her take control, though I felt like I was going to explode at any minute. My balls ached, and I was desperate for relief.

She opened her eyes and leaned forward, resting her hands on my chest as she began riding me. It felt incredible to be so deep inside without any barriers between us. I never went without a condom, but now, I couldn't imagine using one with her now that I knew how amazing it felt.

She bounced harder, increasing her speed as she lined herself up to have my cock rub her clit with each movement. Soon, I felt my orgasm building at the same time her thighs clenched around me as she chased her own.

We both stifled our moans as we climaxed together, the perfect gift that neither of us expected.

Epilogue
Emily
Two Months Later

"You have a Zoom meeting in five minutes," I giggled as Jackson kissed my neck while I sat in front of him on his desk.

"Yeah, but I'm not done with my current assignment."

He rubbed his hands up my thighs and under my skirt.

"Did you lock the door?" I whispered, closing my eyes as I enjoyed his touch.

"Mmmhmm."

His mouth was busy working its way up one exposed thigh before hovering over my pussy.

"Jackson, what if someone logs on early and sees us?"

"I turned the camera off."

"What about the audio?"

"Then I guess you're going to have to be a good girl and be quiet."

The thought of him doing this while on a conference call with the management in the New York office was thrilling and exciting.

"Jackson," I panted heavily as he slid my panties to the side and pulled my body down as he started licking my folds.

My back arched, and I gave up any fight I had a few seconds ago. This felt too good to worry about us getting caught.

I was in full-blown bliss when I heard a man's voice on the computer.

"Hey, Jackson. The rest of the team should be on shortly. I don't see your camera, though."

Jackson pulled away for a second to answer.

"Hey, Beau. I'm eating lunch, so I have it off for now. Not to worry, I'm here and can hear you."

"Sounds good."

Jackson lowered himself back between my legs and started eating me out as if I were a real meal. Other voices soon filled the room, and conversations about different accounts floated around me. I ignored everything that was being said and focused on the way Jackson was flicking my clit with his tongue.

"Yeah, we can discuss the Colbin deal," he agreed, pulling away as he inserted two fingers inside of me. "They're close to coming to a decision."

I was close to coming.

I opened my eyes and watched as Jackson stood above me, his fingers deep inside as he fucked me, a bulge straining against his slacks.

He lifted his other hand and raised a finger to his lips, reminding me to be quiet. Slowly, he pulled his zipper down and then reached in and pulled his thick cock out.

I was so close to coming, and the sight of him pushed me even further over the edge. He kept his rhythm while he fingered me, then rubbed my clit with his thumb until my legs trembled around him.

It was hard to be quiet as I came, but it was even more thrilling to do it while a handful of people were on the Zoom call. As soon as I was finished, Jackson pulled his hand away and motioned for me to turn around.

I stepped to the side, planting my heels firmly on the designer rug, and bent over his desk. He pushed my skirt up and slid his hand over my ass before lining his cock up at my entrance.

"Quiet," he reminded me, leaning in to whisper in my ear.

Then he reached over and turned the audio off for the meeting before he plowed into me. I knew it would be fast and hard, just the way I liked it.

I lifted my ass as he slid inside, plunging into the wetness he'd been licking just a few minutes before. I gripped the desk the best I could as he thrust inside.

Sex with Jackson was beyond amazing, and we got creative with the places we had it. Having three kids and living in one house made it hard to avoid getting caught. Granted, we took full advantage of the time my mom watched them for us, but our appetite for each other required more frequent escapades.

I could feel him tightening inside of me and knew that he was close. I clenched as hard as I could, begging him to come inside me. We decided from the start not to bother with condoms and recently talked about what would happen if something changed and I got pregnant.

While I had two kids already, and Jackson had Sophie, it was different for him because he didn't have a biological child of his own. I was surprised to find that he wanted one, and when I told him I would be open to having another, he started practicing every opportunity he got.

We hadn't talked to the kids about the possibility of them having a new sibling and wanted to give it a little more time before we did, which meant we were still *practicing* for now.

I heard Jackson moan a few seconds later as his balls slapped harder against my ass. It was a good thing he had muted the call after all.

I giggled as he pulled out and stepped away to clean himself off with some tissue. I gave him a quick peck on the lips and then waited until he was situated before I slipped out of the office and went to the bathroom to clean myself up.

When I returned, he was actively engaged in the meeting, with the audio and video turned on. I took my seat at the desk he'd bought for me right after New Years and started working on the plans for us to go to New York next month.

Jackson was still paying the mortgage on Cammy's house and decided to keep it for Sophie. Nothing had been changed other than clearing out Cammy's stuff after Jackson and Sophie went through it. The pictures on the wall were a pleasant reminder of the love and happiness that filled their home before Cammy passed.

We'd taken a few trips to the house as a family, and Sophie was excited to show the girls her bedroom and the treehouse outside that she used to play in. Part of me wondered whether it was best for Jackson to stay in Sugarplum Falls or if he should go back to New York City and let Sophie grow up in the home her mother had created for them.

But then he reminded me that home isn't a place. It's a feeling. As far as our family was concerned, we were all home when we were together.

****

Thank you for reading Emily and Jackson's story! I hope you enjoyed it! If you want more Sugarplum Falls, be sure to check out Sunny's story in Blame It On The Eggnog
https://books2read.com/u/38PPY6

Looking for more holiday romance? Be sure to check these titles out!

Snow Place To Go

https://books2read.com/u/4A560N

A Christmas Wish

https://books2read.com/u/4EKXpE

Holiday Hijinks

https://books2read.com/u/4DP6Ze

<u>Other Books By Samantha Baca</u>

<u>The Haven Brook Series</u>
<u>(small-town romantic suspense):</u>

'Til Death Do Us Part (Haven Brook Book 1)

https://books2read.com/u/m2RJNR

The Cradle Will Fall (Haven Brook Book 2)

https://books2read.com/u/b6O0QE

The Ties That Bind (Haven Brook Book 3)

https://books2read.com/u/mqgoz8

A Very Haven Christmas (Haven Brook Book 4- Novella)

https://books2read.com/u/mvqGjj

Three Strikes, You're Gone (Haven Brook Book 5)

https://books2read.com/u/mvqL2z

The Dark Shadows Series (romantic suspense)

Five Steps Ahead (Dark Shadows Book 1)

https://books2read.com/u/38Q0gO

Ten Seconds Too Late (Dark Shadows Book 2)

https://books2read.com/u/3JRgVB

Against The Clock (Dark Shadows Book 3)

https://books2read.com/u/m2YwoR

Out Of Time (Dark Shadows Book 4)

https://books2read.com/u/4DKMoP

The Stone Creek Series (small-town- novellas)

Chocolate Covered Mistletoe (Stone Creek Book 1)

https://books2read.com/u/3LRk9N

Candy Coated Promises (Stone Creek Book 2)

https://books2read.com/u/mldP5Y

Pumpkin Spiced Possibilities (Stone Creek Book 3)

https://books2read.com/u/bojdwV

<u>Beaumont Creek Series (small town)</u>

Just One Time (Beaumont Creek Book 1)

https://books2read.com/u/3G52zK

Second Chances (Beaumont Creek Book 2)

https://books2read.com/u/4Aj6Z0

Third Time's The Charm (Beaumont Creek Book 3)

https://books2read.com/u/b5lEyG

Four-ever Single (Beaumont Creek Book 4)

Preorder link coming soon

Fifth Wheel (Beaumont Creek Book 5)

Preorder link coming soon

<u>Whiskey Mountain Series (small-town-novellas)</u>

Something To Talk About

https://books2read.com/u/4X62ag

Something To Think About

https://books2read.com/u/3GWAan

Something To Believe In

https://books2read.com/u/3yVzgB

Something To Live For

Preorder link coming soon

<u>Sugarplum Falls Series (Holiday Novellas- can be read as standalone)</u>

Blame It On The Mistletoe

https://books2read.com/u/bw1rqe

Blame It On The Eggnog

https://books2read.com/u/38PPY6

Standalone Books

One Last Wish

https://books2read.com/u/mqg7D9

Finding Love In Apartment 2C (novella)

https://books2read.com/u/bze9aZ

Cocky Counsel: A Hero Club Novel

https://books2read.com/u/31Kzkn

All Is Fair In Food And War (novella)

https://books2read.com/u/bp8qjX

Holiday Books (novellas)

Snow Place To Go

https://books2read.com/u/4A560N

A Christmas Wish

https://books2read.com/u/4EKXpE

Holiday Hijinks

https://books2read.com/u/4DP6Ze

<u>Acknowledgments</u>

As always, I'd like to start by thanking all of the wonderful readers who picked up my book and decided to read it! Thank you! I hope you enjoyed the story and fell in love with the beautiful town of Sugarplum Falls!

To my alpha, beta, and ARC readers—what would I do without you guys?! Honestly, I don't want to know, so promise never to leave me, okay? Okay. Thank you from the bottom of my heart for loving my books and being so eager to start the next one.

My dear family, thanks for the constant support! You'll never know how much it means to me, even if I shout it from the top of a mountain! But let's not try that because we know how well I do in the mountains these days… So maybe just trust me when I say it? Love you!

Tillie—I'm so glad I was able to steal you away again to help me with editing! I LOVE your feedback and seeing your reactions along the way!

My sweet girls, thank you for your constant enthusiasm when you see one of my books or tell people that your mommy writes books. I LOVE your passion for reading and might be a little jealous that your library is now bigger than mine! Keep reading and let those words take you places you've never dreamed of, my loves.

Richard, even with a million other things going on, you always make time for me. Thank you for chasing my dream with me. I know sometimes it feels like a wild ride—and not in the best way—but I promise we'll get where we want to go together. Thank you for everything you do. You're amazing, and I love you more than you could know.

Thank you again for reading this novella! If you've enjoyed it and wouldn't mind leaving an honest review on your favorite platform, I would greatly appreciate it!

About the Author

Samantha lives in the southwest with her husband and two small children after abandoning her childhood dream of living in a cabin in Colorado when she found that she couldn't afford to live there and was deathly allergic to the woods. When she's not writing, she's usually spouting off sarcastic remarks while drinking wine out of a coffee mug to look like a functional adult while chasing down her toddlers. She enjoys spending time with her family, watching reruns of Friends, and the 24/7 flow of coffee that can be found in her veins. Be sure to follow her on social media for updates on what she's working on.

You can find her here:

Facebook: https://www.facebook.com/AuthorSamanthaBaca

Instagram: https://instagram.com/author_samantha_baca

Goodreads: http://www.goodreads.com/authorsamanthabaca

Facebook Reader Group:

https://www.facebook.com/groups/2945710968775398/

Webpage: https://authorsamanthabaca.wordpress.com

Newsletter: http://eepurl.com/g0NcSj

Printed in Great Britain
by Amazon